MISSION 10

LAST STAND

SIGMUND BROUWER

TYNDALE HOUSE PUBLISHERS, INC.
WHEATON, ILLINOIS

Visit the exciting Web site for kids at www.cool2read.com
and the Mars Diaries Web site at www.marsdiaries.com

You can contact Sigmund Brouwer through his Web site at
www.coolreading.com

Designed by Ron Kaufmann

Edited by Ramona Cramer Tucker

ISBN 0-8423-5634-7, mass paper

Printed in the United States of America

08 07 06 05 04 03 02
7 6 5 4 3 2 1

THIS SERIES IS DEDICATED
IN MEMORY OF MARTYN GODFREY.

Martyn, you wrote books that reached all of us kids at heart. You wrote them because you really cared. We all miss you.

CHAPTER 1

Tidal wave!

Not water. But blood. Whooshing down a narrow pipeline.

I knew the rush of blood was out there only because I could hear it surge ahead with each heartbeat—a sound like a distant drum. But I couldn't see anything because I was inside a shiny steel transporter pod, half the size of a pea, carried along by the powerful flow of blood.

Well, actually, it wasn't *me* inside the pod but the miniature robot I controlled through virtual reality. But it *felt* like I was inside the pod. Since my brain waves were connected to the robot, I saw and heard what the robot saw and heard. In turn, the robot responded to my brain waves and moved the way my own body would move.

The robot itself was an incredible piece of machinery. It was a second-generation ant-bot, about one-tenth the size of the original mini-robots. And those first ones were smaller than an ant!

Yet even with being that tiny, there wasn't much room for the robot's arms and legs to move inside the absolute darkness of the pod. There certainly was nothing to see inside. All I could do was wait and listen to the blood outside as the transporter pod moved through the major arteries of the president of the United States of America.

I could picture what was happening, however.

My own human body was strapped motionless in place, just outside the operating room. Signals from my brain were sent to a transmitter, which in turn sent them via X ray to the computer chips of the tiny robot.

Inside the operating room, the president sat calmly in a chair, hooked to heartbeat monitors, waiting for the transporter pod to reach the pacemaker in her heart. Something had caused it to slow down, and the doctors didn't know what. Checking it by robot was much easier on her than having a major operation that would open her chest cavity and keep her in the hospital for weeks.

Just a few minutes earlier, a doctor had injected the tiny pod into an artery in her hip. A beeping locator signal let the doctor know of its progress. As my robot waited, the doctor guided the pod through the president's arteries with a powerful magnet. The inside of the pod was lined with a thin rubber coating so the electrical forces generated by the magnet wouldn't disturb the intricate wiring of the robot. But the X-ray signals could still get through the rubber, and that allowed me to stay in contact with the doctor.

"Tyce," the doctor said, "you're moving toward the lungs now. I'm sorry it's taking so long, but I made a wrong turn at the kidneys. After all, this is the first time something like this has ever been tried."

Although I couldn't see anything, I imagined the walls of the arteries stretching and throbbing with each beat of the heart. I imagined glowing red saucer-shaped platelets swarming just outside my pod.

"Tyce," the doctor continued, "are you ready? I mean,

really ready? We're talking about a human life at stake. And this human happens to be the president of the most powerful country in the world. If she dies, a lot of other people will suffer."

"Yes, sir," I said. "I'm ready."

The doctor had explained it to me earlier. When the pod reached the right place near the president's heart, he would trigger the pod to release some tiny spikes that would secure it to the blood vessel. Then the pod would open, and my robot would seek its target—the pacemaker of the president of the United States.

I'd spent hours going over the model of a pacemaker, studying computer-generated images to give me an understanding of how it would appear to my tiny robot.

"I'm ready," I confirmed. "As soon as the pod opens."

It took the doctor another 30 seconds. "Get ready," he warned.

"Ready," I repeated.

And blood rushed in as the pod cracked open.

Immediately my robot began to sway with the movement of the blood. The president's heartbeat had fallen to 30 beats per minute. One every two seconds. A hard tidal wave rushed over me; then it became relatively calm and I floated in an ebb of blood.

A beat every two seconds. Slower than if she'd been asleep. Her heart wasn't pumping enough blood, and her body desperately needed oxygen. Already some of her major organs had begun to shut down.

My robot was tethered to the inside of the transporter pod by a microscopic strand of titanium. The next heartbeat would pump blood that would shoot me forward until I reached the end of it, like a dog running to the end of its leash.

A light attached to the robot's right arm showed a red glow of blood around it. But if the doctor had placed the pod correctly, the next heartbeat would take me right into the pacemaker and . . .

The robot shot forward as blood gushed again through the artery. Then it stopped hard. I'd hit the pacemaker!

Now my tiny light bounced off the shininess of the pacemaker's plastic. It would have to be enough.

The light showed a small seam. I grabbed it and held on. I needed to be secure before the next heartbeat washed a new wave of blood over me.

The wave came. It tugged at my robot body.

I held.

I climbed farther for another second.

I held. Waited for another rush of blood. Then climbed.

Again and again. Until finally I reached a tiny opening that led into the pacemaker.

I waited for another heartbeat to pass before moving inside.

Once inside, I needed to find a wire that, although nearly invisible to human eyes, would look like a thick rope to a robot this size. The wire sent an electrical current to the pacemaker controls from its power source. It was insulated, so I didn't have to worry about putting my robot in risk of shock, which could also shock my own brain. It was this wire that doctors suspected was loose or frayed, causing the slower heartbeat.

My robot hand finally found the wire. It was so big in comparison that I could barely wrap the robot fingers around it. I grabbed and held tight.

That was my mistake.

I should have been holding something else.

The next wave of blood shifted my robot body.

I forgot to let go of the wire.

It held me briefly, then snapped loose as blood tugged at my robot body. For a moment my robot body swayed. Then it stopped, suspended in blood.

And I realized what had happened.

I'd disconnected the wire that, until then, had just been frayed or loose. All heartbeats of the pacemaker stopped.

"Tyce!" the doctor shouted. "Tyce! What's going on in there? The president is screaming with pain. She has—!" He stopped for a second, then shouted louder. "Tyce! She's collapsed. We can't get a heartbeat on these monitors! Tyce! Tyce Sanders! Do something in there!"

CHAPTER 2

"Can you scratch my back?" I begged my best friend, Ashley. A cast covered my body from my knees all the way up to just below my armpits. The skin beneath my body cast was so itchy I wouldn't have cared if she used a chain saw to get at it.

I'd just finished my virtual-reality simulation, and my heart was still pounding.

"You just killed the first woman president in the history of the United States, and that's the first thing you're going to say for history to record?" Ashley exclaimed, helping me take off my sensory-deprivation helmet.

I rubbed my face where the helmet had pressed for the last half hour. The helmet was designed to make sure no light or sound reached my own eyes or ears during robot control. Even though it was tight enough to be barely comfortable, it was an improvement on the headset and blindfold I had first used to go into robot control, almost four years ago, on my home under the dome on Mars. Of course, with the total backing of the World United Federation after uncovering the plot to kill the Vice-Governors, all of our stuff had been replaced with the best and newest of equipment.

This included updated computer programs to simulate situations where robot control could help the rest of humankind. Things like robot submarines. Robot helicopters. Robot firefighters. And robot surgical units, like the ones used in the virtual-reality medical emergency I had just failed.

I knew a little about the history of computers and how this new ant-bot was technologically possible. The first silicon computer chips—way, way back in the late 1900s—were wafers hardly bigger than a pinkie fingernail. Now those wafers looked like baseball stadiums compared to the modern computer chips, which were tinier than a pinhead. Information pathways were etched on these chips less than a molecule in width. My small robot needed only two chips for all its computing work, and the robot's arms and legs were so tiny that only other miniature robots—guided by human brains—could build them.

Ashley floated beside me, holding my sensory-deprivation helmet by its strap. She had just unhooked me from my robot-control transmitter.

"At least I was able to fix her pacemaker," Ashley said, rubbing in her own success. Her dark almond eyes crinkled as she grinned. "Every time *you* tried, the blood knocked you out of your pod."

OK, so she had me there. Ashley was right. She was a good match for me in virtual-reality skills. Although I wouldn't tell her so outright, secretly I was glad. After all, that was what had brought us together as friends when she'd arrived on the planet of Mars almost four years ago. I'd thought I was the only person in the universe who had a spinal plug to connect with robots. Then I'd discovered that Ashley did too—and that there were many more "pods" of kids like us, scattered around the world and even on a space station rotating the Moon.

But that wasn't the only thing that made us friends. It had helped that we were the only two our age on Mars. Even more, I could trust her. I mean, really trust her. We'd been through a lot of life-and-death adventures together on Mars and then on Earth over the past three years. She had been one of the rare people who hadn't minded hanging out with a crippled kid—a kid who could never remember walking because of an experimental spinal operation gone wrong when he was young.

During the past two and a half years on Earth, as we waited for the orbit rotation of Earth and Mars to line up so that my dad, Chase Sanders, a space pilot, could take us back to Mars, Ashley and I had become even closer. After all, it isn't just any friend who hangs around when you have to spend most of your time visiting doctors and having multiple tests—or up to your eyeballs in a cast. After saving the Vice-Governors' lives, I'd been told it was possible I would be able to walk again. But it could mean losing my ability to control robots through virtual reality.

It sounds crazy, I know, but the choice had been tough. I'd never been able to walk my whole life—but my world, and all my training since I was a kid, had been in virtual reality. It was hard to think about giving that up.

But after a lot of discussions with my dad, my mom, Kristy Sanders, a leading plant biologist still back on Mars, and the Mars director, my doctor and friend Rawling McTigre, I'd decided to go for it. And Ashley had been my biggest supporter, keeping my mind busy—especially over the two months I'd spent in the body cast on Earth and now these almost six months on the spaceship back to Mars.

It was Ashley who had insisted that I try connecting with a robot soon into my recovery after surgery. I'd been too scared to try it by myself. And I'd been surprised—and greatly relieved—when my spinal plug still worked to connect my brain waves to a robot. So at least I knew that part of my life would still work.

But could I walk? Actually be able to take steps on my own, outside of virtual reality with a robot? It had been eight months since my surgery, and I still had to wait and see.

I was glad Ashley was still by my side . . . and that she still had her sense of humor. As annoying as it could be sometimes.

I wrinkled my nose at her, knowing that my small action would speak louder than words.

"There's always tomorrow," Ashley teased, attempting to tuck a strand of her straight, shoulder-length black hair behind her ear. "Give me one more try and—"

I sucked in a breath at the itchiness of my ribs. If only there was room to be able to squeeze my hands inside the cast and scratch, scratch, scratch with my fingernails. Until I'd been put in this body cast, I'd spent my life in a wheelchair. But I'd never once dreamed there would come a day when I'd think a wheelchair was freedom. Yet compared to the prison of this cast, I wondered. . . . Tubes seemed to stick out of me everywhere. The ones I hated the most were those that fed my body wastes into a pouch hidden by my jumpsuit pants.

"This close to Mars," I answered, "we should probably spend more time on the carbon-dioxide generators."

I didn't mean that she or I should hook up to a carbon-dioxide machine, of course. After all, we humans breathe oxygen. But the atmosphere on Mars needed more carbon dioxide, and that's why we were on our way.

"We" meaning 50 kids like Ashley and me who had robot-control capability. Ashley herself had been part of a "pod" of 24 kids who were either orphans or had been stolen from their parents at a very young age. Then, against their will, they'd been given the spinal-plug operations and forced to work like slaves, controlling virtual-reality soldier robots from jelly tubes where they lived night and day.

When I'd first seen the kids in Ashley's pod in Parker, Arizona, I'd felt sick. It wasn't fair that these kids had had their lives stolen from them. Because of the power-hungry Dr. Jordan and the elusive mastermind Luke Daab. Or that some of these kids would never know their parents. All of them had undergone extensive DNA testing to try to reunite them with their parents. The World United Federation had found matches for most of them. Ashley had found her parents during our years on Earth, but that was an entirely different story—one I was going to put in a diary once I had settled in on Mars again. It had been tough for Ashley to say good-bye to her parents, but Ashley knew she would return to Earth after her work on Mars was finished. It wasn't like she would be too lonely. My dad, mom, and I were the closest friends she had, and we'd be with her on Mars.

After hearing about the need for human life to expand to new planets like Mars and the capabilities of the new carbon-dioxide generators to provide an atmosphere in which life could thrive, 50 of the kids had also decided to come—on their own. They were excited about being part of "saving the Earth" in a unique way—by controlling the robots that worked the carbon-dioxide generators.

And now within two days we'd land on the red planet. After a trip of 50 million miles.

But before we did, we all needed as much virtual-reality practice as possible to assemble the parts to the carbon-dioxide generators. On Mars we would be building the real giant gas generators on the surface of the planet.

"I can't give up on this pacemaker thing," Ashley said.

"One of us has got to be able to save her life one of these times. Poor woman must be tired of dying."

The poor woman wasn't real, of course—just a computer model. And one of the many different programs the World United Federation had created for the Mars journey. I couldn't imagine how many millions and millions of dollars had been spent to generate the programs since the technology first became public, after the near-death of the Vice-Governors at their yearly Summit in New York City. But with 50 of us spending six months in space, traveling from Earth to Mars, we needed something to do that could be of good use down the road.

Although the stuff we did to pass time was practical, it didn't feel like work. The virtual-reality simulation programs were fun and good training, and we had plenty of time to read books. Ashley liked fiction; I was really getting into science. Learning about . . .

Ashley poked me. I was spacing out again, mentally writing in my diary. I'd first hated it—when my mom had made me start it as homework almost four years ago on Mars. But now I used it to track my thoughts and think through problems.

"She might be tired of dying in virtual reality," I said, "but here in real life I'm dying to get scratched. Can't you find anything to help?"

Ashley raised an eyebrow and put her hand on her hip in her trademark gesture. "Just another powder injection."

"A wire," I begged. "A stick with sandpaper on the end. Something to rub my skin."

"Powder," she insisted. "I'm your friend and you have strict doctors' orders not to use anything but powder. Scratching skin beneath a cast can lead to sores and infections and scars."

"Powder then." I made a face. Ever since I'd been in the body cast I'd needed someone to inject a special medical powder beneath my cast twice a day. It helped keep my skin dry and also had a numbing effect to get rid of the itching as my body healed from the surgery. But I really, really wanted the feeling of something to scratch at the skin. In one way, it would be great to get out of the cast.

And in another way, I was worried about the day the cast was taken off because if . . .

I stopped my thoughts. I was too afraid to wonder what would happen then.

"You all right?" Ashley asked, catching the expression on my face.

It was hard to fool her.

I grunted, "Fine." Then a sudden headache hit me so hard it felt like a hand grenade had just exploded inside my brain.

Ashley put the helmet in my hand and pushed away. In the weightlessness of outer space, that effort moved her easily toward the hatchway that led out of the computer room to the rest of the spaceship.

She stopped at the hatchway. "Could be worse, you know," she said, looking at me intently. "If you have to be in a body cast, at least it's in a zero-gravity situation."

That's the way the doctors had planned it. Zero gravity meant I could still be mobile. More important, it would give my spinal cord the best situation to repair the nerve splinting they had done. So they'd done my surgery only two months before I left Earth—enough time for them to make sure there were no complications, but not enough time for me to go crazy in Earth's atmosphere.

"You're right." I tried to smile through the incredible headache that gripped my skull. I should have expected it.

These headaches were coming like clockwork, once every four hours. They were lasting longer and longer, some for 10 minutes. Was there something wrong inside my brain? I was scared even to mention them to anyone—much less Ashley or my dad, who would really be worried.

As I spoke to Ashley, I continued to smile to hide the pain. "It could be worse."

But not much. I'd had little headaches before on Mars and on Earth. Ones that were dull and just annoying. But these headaches were different. They'd only begun a few months earlier, halfway through the spaceship trip to Mars. Every day they were becoming more and more intense. I wondered if they would kill me before our fleet of spaceships reached Mars.

And that was only two days away.

CHAPTER 3

The red planet filled much of the view from the observatory. I couldn't believe I'd be home soon. My years on Earth had been so full of adventure that sometimes Mars hadn't seemed real. Only the memories of my mom and my friend Rawling were still vivid.

Funny though, how the more a person does in life, the more it brings good-byes. Good-bye when leaving Mars, then good-bye to friends when leaving Earth. I felt torn between two homes. Back on Earth, it hadn't been easy saying good-bye to my friends Cannon and Nate. And I could tell from the other kids' tears when saying good-bye to their parents that they felt the same. One of our friends, Chad, had changed his mind at the last minute and stayed with his dad, the general who had helped us on Earth. It was the same with the Supreme Governor's grandson, whom Ashley and I had rescued from robot-control slavery.

But what choice did a person have? If baby birds never left the nest, they never learned to fly. All of us had a destiny to follow and . . .

"Science book in your lap but eyes closed and daydreaming, huh?"

I blinked open my eyes. "Uh, hi, Ashley."

"Learning anything?"

"The usual."

"More science?"

"It's interesting," I said.

"Right."

"OK, then," I said. "How bright would it seem to you if you were standing in the center of the sun?"

Although there were other kids on board the ship, she and I were alone in the ship's observatory.

Three hours had passed since I'd wrecked the virtual pacemaker of the virtual president of the United States. My headache was gone. My skin didn't itch quite so bad. And I was floating beneath the eyepiece of a telescope that extended through the upper panels of the spaceship.

It wasn't until I'd spent time on Earth that I realized outer space allowed such an incredibly clear view of the stars and galaxies. On Earth, stars twinkled as the atmosphere bent their light; here on the spaceship, the stars were bright enough against a black background to hurt the eyes.

How could anyone who saw a view like this wonder if God existed? I thought. Space was so big—so endless. And yet so ordered. Although many scientists still insisted that life had come from random chance, I had learned that scientific evidence pointed to what I, Mom, Dad, Rawling, and Ashley believed—that God was the one who'd created everything. And made life possible on Earth. It wasn't just some "energy" that happened to find other "energy" and matter and create itself. God had planned it all—and my life too. When I wondered what would happen to me in the future—if I'd really be able to walk—those were the truths I held on to.

And coming to that realization hadn't been easy. It had taken an oxygen leak in the dome and many other near misses with death to get me to admit—and then accept—a personal relationship with the Creator of the universe.

I grinned and shook my head. Sometimes I could be so stubborn. . . .

"Huh?" Ashley's face was buried in her comp-board, a computer made of a keyboard and screen that folded together.

"If you were standing in the center of the sun, how bright would it be?" I said again.

Ashley looked up from her homework. "Answering that beats trying to figure out Shakespeare. And I know it's a trick question. You wouldn't see a thing. You'd be burned to a crisp. Just like what nearly happened to us because of Luke Daab on the trip to Earth."

Luke Daab . . . the very name made me shiver. Who would think such a mousy-looking guy could cause such big trouble? But because of him and his evil plans we'd been trapped on a runaway spaceship that would have crashed right into the heart of the sun if we hadn't found a way to stop it.

"It's not a trick question," I said, swinging the telescope idly in different directions. "If you could survive in the middle of the sun, how bright would it be on your eyes?"

She paused her typing.

I kept scanning outer space. I blinked as a large, dark object seemed to jump into view. It was another spaceship in our fleet, its circular shape gleaming dully because of light from the sun a couple hundred million miles away. Including manned and unmanned supply vehicles, there were 20 spaceships altogether. All of us were at least 1,000 miles apart—above, below, and to the sides—cruising through the frictionless vacuum of space at 15,000 miles an hour. To assemble this fleet, the expense for Earth had been a huge gamble. But if it paid off, it would change history. And save billions of lives because it would open up a new planet for human inhabitation.

"I want to say it would be dark," Ashley said, her dark eyes squinting further in thought. "Just because you wouldn't ask the question unless it had some kind of weird answer. But on the other hand, maybe you're trying a reverse on me, and you'll laugh if I don't give the obvious answer."

"What's your guess then?" I smirked.

"Dark," she said at first. Then, more emphatically, "No. Bright. I have to go with bright. So bright you couldn't stand it. I mean, the sun's a couple of million degrees. That kind of heat *has* to be bright."

"It's 27 million degrees in the center, 4.5 million degrees halfway to the surface, and only 10,000 degrees on the surface," I said without looking up from the telescope. "That's in Fahrenheit. If you want it in Celsius, the temperatures are—"

"Remind me never to get stuck in a body cast. If all you do is fill your head with useless facts then—"

I must have looked strange to her. To cover my body cast, I wore an extra-large jumpsuit. My legs stuck straight out, unable to move. And I was just floating underneath the eyepiece, my entire body rigid and straight.

I interrupted her right back. "And even with that kind of heat, the sun is pitch black in the center. It would be darker to you than in the darkest cave in the middle of the Earth. No light at all would reach your eyes."

I finally looked away from my telescope and at Ashley. She was smiling.

"OK, you've got me curious," she said. "Why is the center of the sun that dark?"

"First of all, you have to realize how big the sun is," I answered. "Over three-quarters of a million miles across. A person your size weighs about 100 pounds on Earth. On the sun, its force of gravity would make you weigh over two tons."

Her eyes widened in surprise. "Wow! Tyce, something amazing—"

I waved away her awe at my knowledge. "Keep thinking about that gravity. You see, gravity packs all of the atoms of the sun so tightly together that the rays of light don't get a chance to become rays of light. It's like a—"

"Tyce, you don't understand! I think I—"

"Listen to the professor," I said grandly, continuing my lecture. "Think of a big bag jammed with marbles and a little peewee marble trying to squeeze through. That's what an energy ray has to do as it moves away from the center of the sun. The ray bounces from atom to atom as it heads toward the cooler surface. It makes no light. Isn't it cool how God has arranged it? Science has shown that all of the physics laws were predetermined even before the universe began and—"

"Tyce!"

Again I ignored her interruption. Science was fascinating, and I was determined to finish my little story for her. "Getting back to the sun, it takes 100,000 years for a ray to escape the center and reach the edge and finally become a light ray. Then, finally free of the interference of those tightly packed atoms, it zooms to 186,000 miles per second, flashes through space and, in less than nine minutes, travels the 93 million miles to Earth. After waiting 100,000 years to emerge."

Lying motionless in midair, I folded my arms across my chest. "What do you think about that?"

"Interesting," Ashley said in an almost detached tone. I stopped thinking and focused on her. Her eyes were still wide and she was staring at me. "But not as interesting as the end of your right foot."

"Huh?"

She pointed. "Your right foot. While you were talking, I noticed it. That's what I was trying to tell you."

"Is this some sort of trick? To change the subject or something?" I began.

"No," she said. Then a tear rolled down her cheek. "It's not a trick at all."

"I don't get it," I said, suddenly scared. I hadn't had much experience with girls beyond my friendship with Ashley. But I knew enough to realize it's not good when girls start to cry. "What did I do wrong? Is my foot too smelly for you? Is that why you noticed it?"

She began to laugh but kept crying at the same time. "Your toes. Under the sock of your jumpsuit, I saw your toes move while you were talking."

Toes? Move?

I lifted my head and looked down my body. I could see the top of my toes. I watched them closely. *Wiggle,* I commanded my toes. *Wiggle.*

I'd tried that thousands of times growing up. Sitting in my wheelchair, I'd stare at my leg or my foot or my toes and try to move them by concentrating hard. I'd prayed. I'd begged God to let them move. Until years of disappointment convinced me otherwise, I believed that, just once, I could think hard enough to send my lower body a message. To make it listen to me. Or that God would do a miracle and *poof!* I'd be able to walk again.

But nothing had ever happened. Not for a kid whose spinal cord had been damaged when he was barely more than a baby. That was probably one reason it had taken me so long to believe that God not only existed, but he really cared about me.

Except now my toes moved. Just a little. *But they moved!*

"Oh, wow," I said.

Ashley pushed off a wall in my direction. When she reached me, she gave me a hug.

"They did move, didn't they!" she said between a few more tears and giggles.

"Oh, wow," I repeated. And then I began to cry too.

That's how we were when the intercom buzzed. Hugging and crying and laughing.

"Hello?" Ashley said, wiping away her tears.

"Tyce and Ashley . . ."

It was my dad, the fleet's lead pilot.

"Thought I'd find you there," he said. "Look, I need you in the navigation cone. Immediately."

CHAPTER 4

Dad was waiting for us in the navigation cone of our spaceship.

This ship had an identical design to all the other manned ships of the fleet. And while it was a new ship, it was similar to the design of the *Moon Racer,* a ship that had taken us to Earth from Mars three years earlier.

The navigation cone formed the nose of the ship and had a great view. The bulk of the ship, made of a titanium-steel alloy, lay behind it. For maximum protection and less expense, the bunks and work areas had no windows. These rooms were lit by the pale whiteness of low-energy argon tubes inset into the walls. They activated whenever anyone moved into the area.

Essentially, the entire ship was a large circular tube, moving sideways through the vacuum of space. The outer part of this large tube held the docking port, two emergency escape ports, an exercise room, all the passenger bunks, and work-area compartments. The inner part of the circle formed a corridor, which we traveled by grabbing handholds and pushing forward or backward, entering the bunks or work areas through circular hatches with slide-

MOON RACER

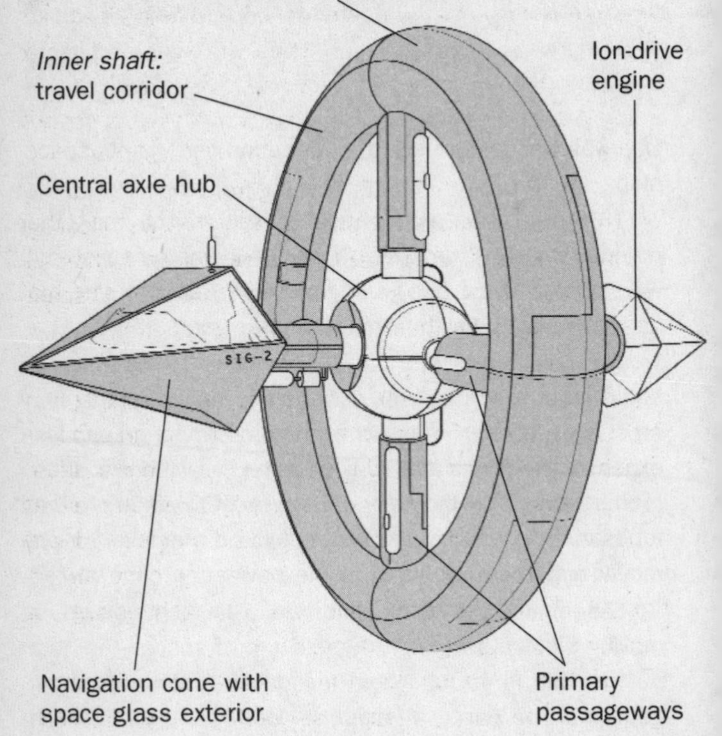
Outer perimeter: docking port, bunkers, work areas, kitchen, exercise room, and emergency escape ports
Inner shaft: travel corridor
Ion-drive engine
Central axle hub
SIG-2
Navigation cone with space glass exterior
Primary passageways

away covers. Also from this corridor, four main hatches led to tubes that extended downward like spokes. They met at a hub in the center so that the four tubes formed an *X* in the center of the giant circle. From the hub at the center where they connected, one short tube led backward to the pyramid-shaped ion-drive engine. Another short tube led forward to this pyramid-shaped navigation cone.

Here the titanium structure of the rest of the ship had been replaced by material that looked and functioned like glass but was thousands of times stronger and more expensive. All the walls of the pyramid were made of this space glass, including the floor. The computer and control console sat on this glass floor, as did the pilot's seat. That's why I liked it so much. Pushing from the hub into the navigation cone made it seem like a person was floating directly into clear outer space. This sensation frightened some people, but because in gravity situations I had spent so much time in a wheelchair, I loved the feeling of freedom.

There was something so awesome about staring into the infinite world of deep space. For me, it always brought more questions about how the matter had come to be in the first place. And more importantly, why? These were God questions. And I still had so many others that I would love to ask him directly. Sitting in the navigation cone always brought those questions back. Yet, strangely enough, it made me feel closer to God too.

Normally I would have pushed into the cone and pressed up against the space glass and stared at Mars. When the sun was on it, it was a beautiful red globe, growing slightly larger each day.

Mars—my home.

But for the moment, I hardly noticed it.

My dad sat in the pilot's seat in front of the control console. He turned as Ashley and I pushed through the hatch into the navigation cone.

Letting our momentum carry us forward, we floated toward him.

People say I look like him—even more so as I've grown older. I have the same dark blond hair he does. My nose and jaws and forehead were still bigger than I wanted them to be, but the rest of my face was starting to catch up. He was big, square and rugged like a football player. It would be great if I kept growing and became his size too. Of course, that's assuming when I got out of my body cast that . . .

I thought of my toes. How they had wiggled. And I wished this were the time to tell Dad.

But his face was set in a frown. I'd save it for later.

"Dad," I said, "we got here as quickly as we could."

He nodded but seemed distracted. He pointed at his computer screen. "I've got something you need to see."

Dad didn't move from in front of the screen to give us a better look. He didn't have to. Not in zero gravity. I hung upside down, above the screen. Ashley stretched horizontally behind him, her face looking over his shoulder.

Each of the spaceships in the fleet sent positioning signals to all the others. On the computer screen, each was a tiny white blip. If I had taken out a pen and connected the outer blips of the formation, I would have drawn a perfect diamond almost filling the screen. Since Dad was the lead pilot, our ship was at the front, with all the others in formation behind. Ten ships, moving majestically and silently in space, thousands of miles apart. Some, like this one, held passengers. The others transported supplies and disassembled carbon-dioxide generators.

"The pattern seems normal to me," I told Dad. I'd been

worried there was trouble with one of the spaceships. Even though the former Manchurian military superpower had lost a series of battles during my Earth years, the World United Federation feared that their Terrataker rebels might try to stop our fleet as a last chance to win their war against the rest of the world.

"It is normal. But watch this." Dad repeatedly punched a button on the console. The computer screen shifted and zoomed out. Again and again. Where once the diamond formation had filled the whole screen, it was reduced to half the screen. Then a quarter. It kept getting smaller and smaller until the blips of all 10 ships merged into one large blip.

Dad shrunk the screen more, and that large blip became almost invisible. Since it was plotted on a computer map of the solar system, the background was studded with the lights of brighter stars.

"Now it's like seeing our space fleet from millions of miles away, right?" I asked.

"Essentially yes, although you need to keep in mind it's a computer simulation of roughly 20 million miles of space. If the scale was truly accurate, you wouldn't even see the blip that represents our fleet." As Dad spoke, he tried to look straight up into my face. He grimaced as his neck twisted. "Let me get you down here on Ashley's level."

He was belted into the chair, so it took him very little effort to pull me beside him and spin my legs back so I was horizontal beside Ashley. My face was on one side of his shoulder. Hers on the other.

He glanced back and forth between Ashley and me. "Keep in mind that our formation is on the right-hand side of the screen, almost at Mars. Now look at the left side of the screen."

"If the scale is 20 million miles," Ashley said, "wouldn't that be about halfway back to Earth?"

"Pretty close," Dad said. He almost touched the screen as he pointed to a star.

Except it wasn't a single star.

"Watch closely again," he said as he hit the console button a few more times. The screen began to zoom in, each time making the white blip bigger. Seconds later the blip began to transform into an entire formation of blips.

"Looks like another fleet of spaceships," I joked. "Weird that from this angle the stars would seem to fit together that way."

"Tyce," Dad said quietly, "it *is* another space fleet."

"What?"

"I've received notice from the World United Federation. Our biggest fear has come true. It's a fleet sent by the Manchurians."

The Manchurians. People who worked alongside Terrataker rebels like Dr. Jordan and Luke Daab, who had tried to kill Ashley, Dad, and me—as well as everyone under the dome on Mars. Rebels who wanted to control the Earth—and everyone living on it—for their own purposes. Who believed in population control, like killing old folks who they believed had "outlived their usefulness" and children who weren't "perfect" physically, instead of developing new places for people to live. Who used kids as slaves to control robots . . .

I shuddered. "Are you sure, Dad?" I asked.

"Take a look at the style of the ships," he replied. "See those markings?"

Ashley and I both looked closer, almost bumping our heads together.

"I believe," Dad said, "they intend to invade Mars."

CHAPTER 5

That night, as usual in zero gravity, I hooked my belt to my sleeping bunk so I wouldn't push off accidentally during the night and float into one of the opposite walls of my room.

I closed my eyes. But I doubted I would fall asleep. Too many thoughts bounced through my head.

If the next headache arrived on schedule, it wouldn't be for another two hours. I was glad for the chance to think without pain. I tried to direct my thoughts toward the Manchurian invasion.

Writing always helped me think, so I began to keyboard a diary entry.

> Our fleet had been assembled over the past two-plus years because of the political situation on Earth that grew steadily worse. Overpopulation was making it extremely difficult to sustain all human life at quality levels. That's why 18 years earlier, the Mars Dome had been established to begin a long-term plan to make the entire planet a place for humans to live outside the dome. If Mars could be made a new colony, then Earth could start

shipping people there to live. This was desperately important. Even now countries verged on war because of the diminishing amount of food and water. Without any help from Mars, millions and millions of people would die from war or starvation or disease.

The silver lining to this cloud was that it had forced all countries to work together for a common cause. They had formed a government, the World United Federation. Not a one-world government, but an umbrella government that let all countries within it remain independent, just like all the different states within the United States worked together.

Except for the Manchurians . . .

Manchuria was a province in China. Although the area itself had not expanded over the last 50 years, its political influence had gone far beyond China to include rebels across the world.

When the World United Federation formed, there were two military superpowers that balanced each other—the United States and Russia. Late in the 20th century, the Russians fell by the wayside as their economy collapsed. China stepped into the vacuum and began to dominate until it almost rivaled the United States. It was a peaceful rivalry until the Manchurians won a civil war in China and took control. Other rebel countries across the world joined the Manchurians so that it was more than China against the World United Federation. Even then the Manchurians had not been powerful enough to risk open war within the World United Federation. But beneath the surface, the Americans were locked in battle against the Manchurian movement for dominance, just like the Cold War that took place between the United States and Russia for 40 years after World War II.

The key now for the Manchurians was to somehow take control of Mars. If they had it, they had leverage against all the other countries in the world. And control now was more important then ever, because it looked like the carbon-dioxide generators the space fleet carried would make it possible for Mars to become a colony in 10 years, instead of the 100 years that had first been projected.

I stopped keyboarding and stared blankly at my computer screen. The Manchurian space fleet should have worried me as I lay floating in the darkness, trying to fall asleep. The Terratakers had been doing everything possible to take over the Mars Project. If the Manchurians were on their way, I had no doubt that it meant Dr. Jordan and Luke Daab were with them.

However, my thoughts kept moving away to something else.

I was too selfish. All I could think about was my toes. How they had wiggled at my command.

It's so easy to take your body for granted. I was just as guilty of this as anyone. In my wheelchair growing up, I was still able to move my arms and hands and head. I never gave much thought to how incredible that was. Your brain sends a command to your hands, and they move. Sometimes I forgot about the miracle of that because I got mad that my legs wouldn't respond. Those were the times that God seemed far away—or rather, the times that I didn't want to talk to him. I was mad at him too, so I ignored him.

Pretended he wasn't there at all. Then a bunch of crises in my life and under the dome had forced me to think about him and discover who he really was. That there was more to life than what we saw on the surface. So I had come to peace, and it was easier to accept how he'd made me unique—even if it meant I was in a wheelchair for life.

And now my toes, for the first time in my life, had moved!

After my surgery, the doctors had refused to make promises. They had said my spine needed to remain immobile to give the nerves a chance to splice completely. That's why I had to be in an almost-full body cast. And the zero gravity of space was an additional plus. But even with all those things going for me, the doctors had eyed one another and said only time would tell if the surgery would work.

But if my toes had moved after all these months in a body cast in space . . .

Lying in the darkness, I began to swell with hope. Maybe when the cast came off, I would be able to walk. To run! What would it feel like? I wondered.

Just as I began to daydream about running through the dome and catching a football thrown to me by Ashley, our ship exploded.

At least that's what it felt like to me.

It took a second to realize the explosion had happened in my head. The headache had arrived early. Even though my eyes were closed in agony, I saw flashing lights and stars, the way it is when you hit your head against something.

And just when I couldn't stand the pain any longer, the flashing lights shut down into total blackness.

CHAPTER 6

I met Dad at breakfast.

Well, it wasn't actually breakfast. Just some liquids in plastic bags called "nutrient-tubes." I drank carefully for two reasons. First, although I had woken up normally when the alarm on my watch sounded, my head still throbbed a little. And second, you don't want to spill anything in zero gravity.

Once Ashley had told me a joke while I was sucking orange juice. I'd laughed and some of the orange juice had gone down the wrong throat tube. Because of my coughing fit, I'd spewed orange juice in all directions.

On Earth that would only mean a sticky mess on the floor, easy to clean up with a couple of wipes.

In zero gravity? Hundreds of tiny orange-juice pellets had immediately spread through the eating room. It had taken 10 minutes to chase them all down, slurping each one back into my mouth as Ashley groaned with disgust.

This morning I was alone in the eating room until Dad pushed through the hatch, holding a folded piece of paper.

"Hey," he said, "Ashley tells me you have some news. Hope it's good. I could use some right about now."

I gave Dad the best smile I could. "My toes wiggled last night. I didn't say anything because the Manchurian fleet . . ."

"Sidetracked us," Dad finished for me, worry spreading across his face. Then his eyes grew wide, as if he'd just realized what I'd said. "Really?" he said slowly. "Your toes actually wiggled? Let's see."

I looked down and focused. They moved again. And even more than last time.

"I can hardly wait to tell your mother!" Dad exclaimed, grinning broadly.

"Me too," I said.

Then Dad's grin faded. "You all right? I thought you'd be a little more excited."

"Just worried," I said, trying to act as nonchalant as possible. I didn't want to concern him further by telling him about my headaches.

Dad nodded and held up the piece of paper. "The other fleet. With all that's happened since you left Mars, I don't blame you for thinking the worst."

It was my turn to nod. If he thought I was worried about the Manchurians, I was going to leave it that way. He had enough to think about as head pilot of the fleet with people like Jordan and Daab on our tail. I'd keep my headaches to myself. Especially since I doubted there was anything he—or anyone else on board the spaceship—could do about them.

"This isn't going to make you any happier either," Dad said. He handed me the paper. "A printout from Rawling."

What kind of bad news would Rawling send? I wondered.

I unfolded the paper. It was an E-mail.

From: "Rawling McTigre" <mctigrer@marsdome.ss>
To: "Chase Sanders" <sandersc@marsdome.ss>
Sent: 04.24.2043, 2:39 P.M.
Subject: Manchurian fleet

Chase (and Tyce),

Last night I received from Earth the same computer information that they indicated was sent to you. I presume you downloaded it immediately and saw that the Manchurian fleet is only a couple of months behind.

My director's report contains some additional information—that military officials on Earth just learned about the fleet themselves. Evidently the Manchurians assembled their own fleet on the dark side of the Moon and launched it in secrecy.

So that explains it, I thought. Why no one—not even the higher-ups on Earth—seemed to know about the fleet until now.

Rawling's E-mail went on:

However, don't worry. Because you'll be arriving first, we should have ample time to set up the surface-to-space missile system you are bringing with you.

See you in two days. Stay in touch—and God bless your journey!

Rawling

P.S. In the meantime, Kristy sends you and Tyce and Ashley all her love. She can't wait to see you!

I was glad to know Mom was thinking about me, just like I was thinking about her. When I didn't have to worry about killer headaches and a killer Manchurian fleet, of course.

"I don't get it," I said, reading the E-mail twice. "It was well publicized that our fleet was carrying atomic missiles—in fact, enough to repel more than 10 Manchurian fleets—to protect Mars against future invasions. The whole point was to make sure the Manchurians didn't even try. So what do they think they can accomplish?"

"Rawling will give us all the information we're cleared to receive when we get to Mars," Dad said. He squeezed my shoulder lightly. "And just so you'll relax, Rawling has a good point. We do have a lot of time to set up our defenses before the other ships arrive."

"Maybe they have long-range weapons on their spaceships," I put in. I'd learned from experience that you never knew what the rebels were up to. "Maybe they'll nuke the dome before our weapons can nuke them."

"Maybe," Dad said quietly.

I studied his face. "You don't look worried."

"Tyce, ever since the Mars Dome was established 18 years ago, it hasn't needed weapons to protect itself from outer-space invasion. So tell me why Mars is suddenly considered valuable enough to be attacked."

"The carbon-dioxide generators," I said. It was an easy answer. That was the whole purpose of the fleet. Carbon dioxide meant that plants could grow. Growing plants produced oxygen. Eventually Mars would have enough atmosphere to be a new colony. "Now that there are enough robot-control kids, we can assemble them and begin establishing an atmosphere where plants can grow and eventually animals and people can live. And that means the colonization of Mars can take place that much faster."

"Exactly. If the Manchurians fire atomic weapons on Mars, it will destroy the very thing they want. So they won't. The only way Mars is worth anything to them is if they can land and take over the dome intact. But there's no way they can land once our surface-to-space missile system is in place. And we've got plenty of time to get it ready." Dad patted my leg. "No worries, then, right?"

I hardly heard him.

"Tyce? Tyce?"

I was staring at my left leg. The one he had just patted.

"Tyce?" he asked one more time.

I looked up at my dad, hardly daring to believe. "It's the strangest thing, Dad," I said. "I think I felt that."

"I'm not sure what you're talking about."

"The bottom of my leg. Where you touched me."

"Here?" Dad grabbed my calf and squeezed.

It felt like electricity running through my body—good, tingling electricity. "Yes! There!" I'd never felt any sensation in my legs before!

Dad high-fived me. Except we slapped palms so hard that it drove us apart in the zero gravity. Seconds later, Dad banged into one wall. I banged into another.

And all we did was grin at each other.

If only the chance to walk was all I had to worry about in the next few months . . .

CHAPTER 7

That night, on the final hours before our approach to Mars, I was alone in the navigation cone, watching the planet loom closer and closer. I'd be back on the red planet within 24 hours.

Dad and everyone else on the spaceship were asleep. That meant the ship was on autopilot, so I had the navigation cone to myself.

I should have been asleep too, but another killer headache had struck. Not bad enough to knock me out this time, which would have been a mercy. Instead it had throbbed for about a half hour, leaving me dizzy and unable to sleep.

Usually in my quiet hours I wrote in my diary on my comp-board. So I had taken it to the navigation cone with me.

I had written a little.

I had dimmed all the lights and stared out into space. Through the glass it felt like I could reach out and touch Mars. And what a glorious sight! I was finally almost home—after a long three years.

Rawling had reported a huge dust storm, and it was just settling. As light from the sun behind the spaceship hit the planet at the right angle, I watched the horizon of Mars spin into sight.

It brought me Mount Olympus, its huge extinct crater sticking out of the dust storm. The mountain itself was bigger than Colorado and reached 15 miles into the sky.

I kept watching, without feeling sleepy at all.

The beauty made me sad, in a way. Because I wondered if there was a tumor or something in my brain to cause these headaches. Was I going to die? Four years ago, when the oxygen level dropped in the dome, the thought of dying really scared me. Although Mom kept telling me that God was with us, that he cared and had our futures in mind, it was hard for me to believe it. It was *her* faith, not mine. But after that brush with death—and many more in all Ashley's and my adventures—I'd learned to trust that we had souls and that our souls belonged home with God. Now the thought of dying wasn't so scary anymore because I knew where I was going. To heaven, instead of some weird, dark void that I'd believed in before. But I still didn't want to die. After all, I was only 17 years old.

Would this be the last time I'd see something as incredible as Mars with the sun warming it?

To take my mind off my thoughts, I turned to my compboard.

But instead of writing, I found myself reading the first entry I had ever put in my diary. It brought back a lot of memories, reminding me of how I'd first learned of my robot-control abilities.

> 06.20.2039 A.D. Earth calendar.
>
> It's been a little more than 14 years since the dome was established in 2025. When I think about it, that means some of the scientists and tekkies in

the dome were my age around the year 2000, even though the last millennium seems like ancient history. Of course, kids back then didn't have to deal with water shortage wars and . . . an exploding population that meant we had to find a way to colonize Mars.

Things have become so desperate on Earth that already 500 billion dollars has been spent on this project, which seems a lot until you do the math and realize that's only about 10 dollars for every person on the planet.

Kristy Sanders, my mom, used to be Kristy Wallace until she married my father, Chase Sanders. They teamed up with nearly 200 men and women specialists from all countries across the world when the first ships left Earth. I was just a baby, so I can't say I remember, but from what I've been told, those first few years of assembling the dome were heroic. Of course, now we live in comfort. I've got a computer that lets me download e-entertainment from Earth by satellite, and the gardens that were planted when I was a kid make parts of the dome seem like a tropical garden.

It isn't a bad place to live.

But now it could become a bad place to die. . . .

Let me say this to anyone on Earth who might read this. If, like me, you have legs that don't work, Mars, with its lower gravity pull, is probably a better place to be than Earth.

That's only a guess, of course, because I haven't had the chance to compare Mars' gravity to Earth's gravity. In fact, I'm the only person in the entire history of mankind who has never been on Earth.

I'm not kidding.

You see, I'm the first person born on Mars. Everyone else here came from Earth nearly eight Martian years ago—15 Earth years to you—as part of the first expedition to set up a colony. The trip took eight months, and during this voyage my mother and father fell in love.

I smiled. I'd forgotten about that. Back when Mom and Dad first came to Mars, the trip from Mars to Earth had taken eight months. And, in just 18 years, scientists had been able to take two months off that time. We were really speeding through space now!

I went back to my first diary entry.

Mom is a leading plant biologist. Dad is a space pilot. They were the first couple to be married on Mars. And the last, for now. They loved each other so much that they married by exchanging their vows over radio-phone with a preacher on Earth. When I was born half a Mars year later—which now makes me 14 Earth years old—it made things so complicated on the colony that it was decided there would be no more marriages and babies until the colony was better established.

What was complicated about a baby on Mars?

Let me put it this way. Because of planetary orbits, spaceships can only reach Mars every three years. (Only four ships have arrived since I was born.) And for what it costs to send a ship from Earth, cargo space is expensive. Very, very expensive. Diapers, baby bottles, cribs, and carriages are not exactly a priority for interplanetary travel.

I did without all that stuff. In fact, my wheelchair isn't even motorized, because every extra pound of cargo costs something like 10,000 dollars.

Just like I did without a modern hospital when I was born. So when my spinal column twisted funny during birth and damaged the nerves to my legs, there was no one to fix them. Which is why I'm in a wheelchair.

It could be worse, of course. On Earth, I'd weigh 110 pounds. Here, I'm only 42 pounds, so I don't have to fight gravity nearly as hard as Earth kids.

I had written that when I had barely turned 14 in Earth years. I knew now, of course, that the spinal damage hadn't been an accident. But a lot of things had happened since that first diary entry. On Mars, Terratakers had tried taking over the dome. They'd tried to fake evidence of an ancient civilization and then attempted to gain control of a space torpedo that would let them dominate the Earth. And on Earth, they'd tried to kill all the Vice-Governors of the World United Federation. They'd forced us robot-control kids to become an army of soldier robots.

And in the middle of all that had been my only journey away from Mars.

I saw the entry I'd written during the space trip to Earth nearly three years earlier, and I remembered the incredible feeling of homesickness.

A little over two weeks ago, I was on Mars. Under the dome. Living life in a wheelchair . . . Then, with the suddenness of a lightning bolt, I discovered I would be returning to Earth with Dad as he piloted this spaceship on the three-year round-trip to Earth and back to Mars. . . .

I'd been dreaming of Earth for years.

After all, I was the only human in the history of mankind who had never been on the planet. I'd only been able to watch it through the telescope and wonder about snowcapped mountains and blue sky and rain and oceans and rivers and trees and flowers and birds and animals.

Earth.

When Rawling had told me I was going to visit the Earth, I'd been too excited to sleep. Finally, I'd be able to see all the things I'd only read about under the cramped protection of the Mars Dome, where it never rained, the sky outside was the color of butterscotch, and the mountains were dusty red.

But when it came time to roll onto the shuttle that would take us to the *Moon Racer,* waiting in orbit around Mars, I had discovered an entirely new sensation. Homesickness. Mars—and the dome—was all I knew.

Dozens of technicians and scientists had been there when we left, surprising me by their cheers and affection. Rawling had been there, the second-to-last person to say good-bye, shaking my hand gravely, then leaning forward to give me a hug.

And the last person?

That had been Mom, biting her lower lip and blinking back tears. It hurt so much seeing her sad—and feeling my own sadness. I'd nearly rolled my wheelchair right back away from the shuttle.

Three years—at that moment—seemed like an eternity. I knew that if an accident happened anywhere along the 100 million miles of travel to Earth and back, I might never see her again. Mom must have been able to read my thoughts because she'd leaned forward to kiss me and told me to not even dare think about staying. She'd whispered that although she'd miss me, she knew I was in God's hands, so I wouldn't be alone. She said she was proud of me for taking this big step, and that she'd pray every day for my and Dad's safe return.

The first few nights on the spaceship had not been easy. All alone in my bunker I had stared upward in the darkness for hours and hours, surprised at how much the sensation of homesickness could fill my stomach.

Who would think that a person could miss a place that would kill you if you walked outside without a space suit. . . .

Since that journey to Earth, these three years had passed.

While battling the Manchurian threat on Earth, the World United Federation had also decided to send us home, back to Mars. It helped that world opinion had shifted heavily to supporting Phase 2 of the Mars Project. So while we waited for the right travel window—for the Earth and Mars to line up in their closest orbit positions—a massive fleet was organized, with updated equipment. And all of us kids with robot-control capabilities were trained to assemble the carbon-dioxide generators.

As for me, a few birthdays had passed, and I was 17 now. I'd seen robot-control technology get better and better.

In fact, in comparison to some of the kids just learning, I was considered an old pioneer of robot control. Just like Ashley.

Yet, exciting as Earth was, I always missed Mars.

Our fleet was so close now—that after three years—within 24 hours I would finally be back.

Home.

Where now it looked like immediately I'd have to help start a defense against the first attempted planetary invasion in the history of humankind.

CHAPTER 8

We didn't land on Mars.

Instead, Dad hooked up our spaceship to the Habitat Lander, a shuttle permanently parked in orbit around Mars. The shuttle was designed to take passengers and equipment down to Mars from the larger spaceships that arrived from Earth.

While it was routine, it was still tricky. If Dad came into the friction of Mars' atmosphere too steeply, the heat would overcome the disposable heat shield and burn the shuttle to cinders. Too shallow, and the Habitat Lander would bounce off the atmosphere toward Jupiter.

Because of my body cast, I was the last one to get strapped in. But at least we were still in low gravity. I wasn't looking forward to being on the surface, when people would have to move me around like a piece of furniture.

By now Dad, Ashley, me, and all the other kids in the shuttle knew each other very well. Traveling through space for months in a vehicle with as much living space as a house would do that.

"Ready, guys?" Dad asked.

There were a few cheers and nods. I looked at all the

faces around me. All these kids had become my friends over the past several years since Ashley and I had helped rescue them. Some, like Joey, seemed nervous. Others, like Michael and Ingrid, looked excited. I reminded myself that except for Ashley and Dad, none of them had been on the red planet before.

Dad hit a few buttons. The hatchway between the shuttle and our spaceship sealed. The Habitat Lander's rockets fired softly, and the shuttle moved away from the spaceship. The spaceship would stay in orbit until the return trip to Earth.

Five minutes later, Dad aimed the nose of the Habitat Lander at the top of Mars' atmosphere.

I knew that a lot of people from the dome would be outside in a platform buggy—four wheels that support a deck, covered by a dome—watching the night sky anxiously for the brightness of our approaching shuttle. The supplies that came with our fleet were crucial to their survival.

If the Habitat Lander crashed, our deaths would be quick and theirs a lot slower.

I prayed, taking comfort in knowing that because of God's love for us, death isn't the worst thing that can happen to a person.

And then the bumping began as we hit the top of the atmosphere.

Dad had warned us to expect a roller-coaster ride, and he was right.

First came the tumbling around as the atmosphere thickened. Loud screaming filled the air inside the shuttle. But it wasn't any of us. It was the shrieking of the heat shield against the intense friction of Mars' atmosphere.

Next came a *clunk* and the dropping of the heat shield.

Then the *pop* of opening parachutes. It felt like a giant hand had just jerked us upward. That's when I got my first reminder of gravity after six months of weightlessness.

The roar of the retro-rockets guided our landing.

And finally, a soft *bump* as we landed.

The shuttle exploded with cheers.

I was home.

"Tyce?"

"Mom!"

Boy, did she look good. Her thick, dark hair was still cut short, like an upside-down bowl, but this time she'd carefully styled it. For the first time I saw a streak of gray.

Lying on my back on the floor of the platform buggy, I grinned at her, despite how dumb I felt.

Although she was smiling, her eyes were searching me.

It had taken at least a half hour for Ashley and Dad to get me in a space suit so I could be transported from the shuttle to the platform buggy. Once inside the safety of the mini-dome of the platform buggy, I'd removed my space helmet.

"Tyce!" Mom exclaimed again. Seeing me in a body cast was no surprise to her, I could tell. We'd been able to send E-mails back and forth the whole time I was in space. She leaned down quickly, then hesitated.

I guessed what she was thinking. That maybe after three years I was too grown-up to be affectionate. Especially in front of all the other kids in the platform buggy.

"Mom! Don't I get a hug?" I said enthusiastically.

Her lips curved in a big grin and she hugged me as best

as she could. Even though I was in a body cast wrapped in a space suit, that hug felt great.

When she let go of me, there was a single, shiny trail of a tear on her cheek. "I'm glad you're home," she said.

"Me too."

Mom stood and hugged Dad too, then kept holding on to his hand. This time seeing their embrace didn't bug me, as it had earlier times when Dad had come home to Mars. It was good to see them together again.

My homecoming on Mars would have been perfect. I saw Flip and Flop, the two Martian koalas I'd rescued from death. It was great being in my own bed. The other kids had settled into their temporary quarters. And it felt very right being with both Mom and Dad again.

Yes, my homecoming would have been totally perfect.

Except for an emergency air leak that threatened to kill everyone under the dome the next morning.

CHAPTER 9

Just after breakfast, I was in a wheelchair in Rawling McTigre's office. It had been great to see his smiling face as soon as I was carried into the dome.

Already I missed zero gravity. The seat back of the wheelchair had been tilted back so my body could recline. Before, when I was in a regular wheelchair without a body cast, at least I could wheel myself around the dome. Now, lying close to horizontal with the cast holding my body rigid, I was totally dependent on other people to move me.

Which was why I was in Rawling's office, where the walls still displayed framed paintings of Earth scenes like sunsets and mountains. I knew Rawling hated the paintings because of what they stood for—that the previous director, Blaine Steven, had used valuable and expensive cargo space to bring such things to Mars for his office. And because of his role in almost killing 180 people under the dome during the oxygen crisis, Steven was still in a World United Federation prison on Earth. But he didn't seem to mind. At least he was safe from the Terrataker rebels who had threatened to kill him.

So why were the paintings still there? I grinned. It was

typical of Rawling to take his responsibilities so seriously that he didn't even take the time to remove the paintings. After all, he was the current director of the Mars Project and also one of only two medical doctors under the dome.

"How long?" I asked—for the 12th time in the last few minutes. Rawling had just passed an X-ray wand over me. On the floor was the lead shield that he'd wrapped around the parts of my body that weren't being X-rayed.

"Just waiting for the film to print out. I'll compare it to the doctor's notes that were e-mailed from Earth. Then, finally, I'll be able to give you an answer. I refuse to guess until then."

For me, Rawling was a mixture of older brother—in his late-forties, much older!—buddy, teacher, and doctor. Rawling had worked with me for hours every day ever since I was eight years old, training me in a virtual-reality program how to control a robot body as if it were my own. His short, dark hair was even more streaked with gray than I remembered. His nose still looked like it had been broken once, which it had. He'd been a quarterback at his university back on Earth when he was younger, and his wide shoulders showed it.

"I think it's finished printing," I said rather impatiently.

"Old age has made you cranky, huh?" he replied wryly.

He still had the same dry sense of humor I remembered. Although 17 was a lot older than when I'd last seen him, it didn't seem like three years had passed. It felt so good to be around him again.

"No, this body cast," I threw in. I was already feeling itchy, and it wasn't even close to time for the body powder.

Rawling leisurely got out of his chair, grinning because he knew I was impatient. He read the X-ray film, then looked up at me.

"Well?" I said.

"Well, what?" he threw back.

"Lost your eyesight since I was last here?" I knew him well enough to tease him. "Need bifocals?"

"Ouch, not even funny," he said. "Because it's true." And laughed. He scanned the medical charts from Earth again. "Your dad must be exhausted. How many shuttle trips are he and the other pilots making?"

"Quit stalling." I knew Rawling already knew. Each shuttle trip took two hours. Dad had to make one shuttle trip for each spaceship but could only do five trips per day. Ours was the only one that had been unloaded last night, since it was so late in the evening. Today some of the passenger spaceships would be unloaded. For the passengers in the other spaceships, one extra day in space wouldn't seem too long, not after the length of the trip. After that, Dad would bring down the equipment and supplies from the unmanned ships. And then the major work would begin. Assembling the carbon-dioxide generators. In the meantime, the other kids were getting a tour of the dome and settling into their new home.

"Stalling?" Rawling asked as innocently as possible. "You accuse *me* of stalling?"

"When can I get the body cast off?"

He grinned and read the X-ray papers one more time. I tried to grab them from him, but he was just out of reach. My arms flailed.

"You can feel your leg and wiggle your toes, right? That's good news."

I groaned. "Come on, Rawling. I already showed you. It's no fun in this body cast. When can we get rid of it?"

Suddenly serious, he scratched his chin. "The X rays show something strange here. At the bottom of your spine.

If I didn't know better, I'd say it was an implanted pacemaker. Except smaller."

"I know what it is. It sends out small electrical impulses that are supposed to help the nerves splice better."

"I don't see mention of it on the charts."

"Well," I said, "that's what one of the doctors told me. All I care about anyway is getting this cast off. When!"

He grinned again. "Tomorrow."

"All right!" I said.

And that's when the dome horns began to scream.

We both knew what it meant. The horns blew for only one reason.

"Oxygen alert!" he shouted above the horns. "Got to go!"

He did.

Seconds later he reappeared with a mask and oxygen tube. He strapped the mask over my face. "If you can't breathe," he shouted, "all you need to do is twist the top of the tube to release the oxygen!"

All across the dome everyone else was doing the same thing. It had been drilled into us again and again. It was the first thing new arrivals learned. When the horns signal an oxygen emergency, go for an oxygen tube. There were at least two in every living area. And dozens and dozens of others scattered across the dome. It meant that anybody at anytime could reach one within 10 seconds of hearing the sirens. Each tube had enough oxygen to last 30 minutes.

"Get one for you too!" I yelled at Rawling. Not that he was likely to forget.

He nodded. "Got to go!"

With that, he was gone.

CHAPTER 10

Ashley rescued me.

Not that I was dying, but it was very frustrating to be stuck in Rawling's office in a body cast in a wheelchair with loud horns vibrating your head and an oxygen mask on your face.

She ran in, her black hair flying around the edges of her own mask. "Rawling said you'd be here!" The only way to communicate was by shouting from beneath the mask. "You all right?"

I nodded. "What's happening?"

"Something punctured the dome!"

"Big hole?"

"The size of a baseball. You should have seen the stuff getting sucked through the hole!"

I could imagine it. The dome was made of a thick, black glass and was powered by huge solar panels hung right below the roof. The dome was pressurized, of course, so air would have escaped through that hole with hurricane force.

"Can you take me out there?" I yelled.

"What?" Ashley exclaimed above the horns.

"Can you—"

I stopped shouting. The horns had finally quit. Someone must have been able to put an emergency patch over the hole. Suction from the outer atmosphere would keep it in place while it was permanently repaired.

I smiled weakly as we both removed our masks. "Can you take me out there?"

"Sure," she said. "But how about you leave this body of yours behind for now."

I knew exactly what she meant. I looked at my watch. "Good idea," I answered. "We've got time."

"Time before what?"

I didn't answer. My next headache was scheduled to arrive in exactly an hour.

"I'll explain when I can," I promised. "Trust me, all right?"

I was excited. You see, when I'd had the surgery to see if I could walk again, the doctors hadn't been sure if I could keep my robot-control capabilities or not. I'd been the first human to have the initial operation, when I was too young to remember. A special rod, hardly thicker than a needle, had been inserted directly into my spinal column, just above the top of my shoulder blades. From that rod, thousands of tiny biological implants—they look like hairs—stick out of the end of the needle into the middle of my spinal column. Each fiber transmits tiny impulses of electricity, allowing my brain to control a robot's computer.

That means I actually see and hear what the robot sees and hears.

I can move the robot's body with my own brain waves, as if I were directing my own body.

And yes, it is cool.

But what wasn't so cool was that something had gone wrong in the surgery and had taken away my ability to walk. When the neurosurgeon inserted the rod into my spine, he'd accidentally cut some of the nerves that went to my legs. Ashley and the other kids, who had the operation later on Earth, didn't have the same problem. They could walk *and* control robots. Now the doctors were hoping that the damage from my initial surgery could be repaired and that I'd be able to do the same thing.

After wheeling me to the computer room, Ashley hooked me to the X-ray transmitter that would put me in contact with my robot, which had already been unloaded and was parked at the far end of the dome.

Ashley ran me through the checklist. Although I had gone into robot control thousands of times—here on Mars and during my couple of years on Earth—I always went through the checklist. Rawling had told me it was like flying a plane. Before you use the equipment, make sure it won't fail.

There were three extremely important things to robot control. One, never allow the robot to have contact with electrical sources. If the robot was electrocuted, it could do serious damage to my own brain. Two, disengage instantly at the first warning of any damage to the robot's computer drive. My brain circuits worked so closely with the computer circuits that harm to the robot computer could scramble my own brain circuits. And third, make sure the robot is at full power and unplugged from the electrical source charging it.

"Check, check, and check," I said. "I'm ready for the helmet."

She lowered it on my head, then snapped the visor in place. Each of us kids had a custom-built helmet. The visor was padded on the inside to fit securely against our faces and block out all light and sound.

My world instantly became black. The only sound was the faint *whoosh, whoosh* of my heartbeat.

In the darkness I gave a thumbs-up, knowing Ashley was waiting for the signal that I was ready.

I waited too. For a familiar sensation, as if I were falling, falling, falling off an invisible cliff in total blackness.

The sensation came.

And I fell, fell, fell. . . .

CHAPTER 11

At the entrance to the dome, light entered the video lenses of my robot where it was parked. Those light waves were transferred by optical cable to the robot's computer. The computer translated those signals and beamed them by remote X rays to the computer that was attached to my spinal plug. The signals then entered my brain as if light had gone through my own eyes.

Through the robot, then, I saw movement everywhere just inside the entrance of the dome. The emergency patch had stopped most of the immediate air loss, but repair crews now had to go outside. Nearby, 10 men and women, geared up in space suits, carried various pieces of equipment as the inner door of the entrance slid open.

If you can picture an igloo large enough to fit 10 people, with that short rounded tunnel sticking out in front, you'll have a good idea of what the entrance to the dome looks like.

In our case, there are two large sealed doors to the tunnel. The outer door leads to the surface of the planet. The inner door leads to the inside of the dome. Between those doors is a gap about twice the length of a platform buggy, where one of them was parked.

As I watched, all 10 crew members climbed the ladder and entered the mini-dome of the platform buggy. The inner door closed and sealed the dome again.

The outer door opened. Instantly the warm, moist, oxygen-filled air from the tunnel turned into white, ghostly vapor and escaped into the cold Martian atmosphere. There was no danger to the rest of the dome, of course, because the inner door was still sealed to keep the dome's air from escaping.

The platform buggy rolled out onto the surface of the planet.

As the outer door began to shut again, another crew member, who had already been outside, stepped into the tunnel chamber. He moved slowly because his bulky space suit made him clumsy. When the outer door sealed shut, he hit a button to open the inner door. A brief puff of vapor showed where Martian air was asborbed into the dome air.

I guessed this crew member had been the first one out there to survey the situation.

I was curious to know what could have penetrated the dome and caused the leak. So I commanded the robot to roll forward.

The man kept walking away, so I sped up to get his attention. It didn't take much extra speed. His space suit slowed him down considerably.

He didn't see me so I tapped him on the shoulder with the titanium robot fingers.

I know I looked strange to him. My robot's lower body was much like my wheelchair. Instead of a pair of legs, though, an axle connected two wheels. The robot's upper body was a short, thick hollow pole, with a heavy weight to counterbalance the arms and head. At the upper end of the pole was a crosspiece to which the arms were attached. Four video lenses at the top of the pole served as eyes. Three tiny microphones, attached to the underside of the video lenses, played the role of ears, taking in sound. A speaker produced sound that would allow me to make my own voice heard, though it always sounded more tinny and mechanical coming from the robot.

The crew member tilted his face toward me. I didn't see it. Space-suit helmets have extremely dark visors.

"Hello," I said. "I am Tyce Sanders. What happened out there?"

The man stopped walking immediately. Now that I had his attention, I waited for him to pull off his helmet. After all, he was in the dome now. He didn't have to worry about the Martian atmosphere.

Instead, he did something strange. Still wearing his space suit, he wriggled his right arm free. The empty sleeve of his space suit hung at his side, but his right arm remained against his body inside the space suit, as if he were searching desperately for something.

"Hello," I repeated more slowly, just in case he hadn't understood me the first time. "What happened out there?"

I never got an answer.

The man looked at me and then pressed something inside his suit.

Instantly it seemed like a baseball bat had slammed against the side of my head.

Not the robot's head. But my head. Where I was lying in my body cast in the computer room.

I screamed at the incredible pain but didn't hear anything because my helmet blocked all sound.

I screamed and screamed until, mercifully, the pain inside my brain must have knocked me totally unconscious.

CHAPTER 12

"Here's what's strange about the hole in the dome," Dad said the next morning.

The pain from my headache had been so intense that I hadn't even woken up until afternoon the day before. And then I'd had to just lie there and rest, until Mom and Dad came to get me to take me to our mini-dome.

Now the three of us—Mom, Dad, and I—were sitting in the small eating area of our mini-dome. Our mini-dome, like everyone else's, had two office-bedrooms with a common living space in the middle. But Mom and Dad weren't able to use their second room as an office because it had become my bedroom. We didn't need a kitchen, because we never had anything to cook. Instead, a microwave oven hung on the far wall. It was used to heat nutrient-tubes, or "nute-tubes," as we called them for short. Another door at the back of the living space led to a small bathroom. It wasn't much. Compared to Earth homes, our mini-dome had less space in it than two average bedrooms.

"Head height," Mom said, sipping on real Earth coffee. I'd brought some back for her, knowing how much she liked it. "No asteroid would come in at that level. I also heard the clean-up crew didn't find anything inside to show what had hit the dome with such impact. So what could have caused it?"

Dad grinned. "It's obvious Tyce got his brains from you."

She kissed his cheek. "And his good looks from you."

"Please," I said, from the horizontal discomfort of my wheelchair. "I feel lousy enough in this body cast. Then to have you two mooning over each other like high school sweethearts . . ."

They both laughed. They knew I didn't mind that much.

Dad took a slurp of his coffee. "Rawling tells me the hole was a perfect circle."

"Not an accident?" I said.

Dad shook his head. "Not an accident. An explosive device is Rawling's best guess."

"But who would do it?"

"That's another weird thing. The dome's mainframe automatically keeps a time log. It doesn't appear that anyone left the dome. It's like someone had been camping out there, waiting to somehow punch the hole."

Dad paused. "That's why Rawling would like to send you and Ashley out there to look around."

He grinned at the frown on my face. "Don't worry, Tyce. Rawling can wait until after your body cast is removed."

"You're not going to like what you see, Tyce," Rawling said gently, a couple of hours after breakfast. "Over eight months your muscles will have wasted away."

I lay facedown on a cot in the small, sterile, square medical room. A zipper down the back and one on each side held the body cast together.

"Didn't have much on my legs to begin with," I answered. "And I'll close my eyes if I don't like the rest of what I see."

Although my words were brave, my stomach had the willies.

"I'm also saying that without healthy muscles, you can't expect to roll off this bed and walk out the door. It's going to take some work before you find out if the operation was completely successful."

Different doctors had already warned me a dozen times that it would take a lot of painful physical therapy and endless hours of exercise. That didn't matter. If I could walk, I'd gladly pay that price a million times over.

"I'm ready, Rawling. Please, please, please, just unzip this stupid thing. I want out."

I heard him unzip the left side of the body cast. He spoke casually. "Ashley says she found you in the computer lab yesterday. Screaming. And then you passed out, and she couldn't wake you up for several hours. Plus your robot was abandoned at the entrance to the dome. Care to tell me about it?"

I took a deep breath. "It was a bad headache that disconnected me. Don't tell Mom or Dad. I don't want them worried. I'm sure the headaches will go away."

Another zip. *"Headaches?* You've had more than one? Tell me as your doctor, not as a friend you don't want to worry."

I told him. All of it.

He unzipped the final panel of the body cast. "Have you had trouble with your vision?"

"No," I said. "Just headaches."

"At least that probably eliminates a tumor or something really bad. Let's look into it once we get this done."

He lifted off the back and both sides of the body cast.

Cool air hit my skin. I felt him place something over the middle of my body.

"What was that?" I asked.

"A towel. It's very encouraging that you felt it. It confirms that the splicing of your spinal nerves was successful."

I wanted to sing with joy—or, even better, dance. But I figured that would take a while. If it was possible . . .

"Keep the towel in place while I roll you over and off the front piece of the body cast," Rawling said. "Then I'll help you sit."

I was about to answer when someone knocked loudly on the door.

"Hang on," Rawling called. "Two minutes."

"It's me," a voice said. My dad's voice.

"Want him in?" Rawling asked.

"Sure. As soon as you have me sitting."

That took another minute.

And that's how Dad found me. On a chair. Sitting. Wrapped in a towel around my midsection. With a blanket around me to keep me warm.

"Toothpick, huh," I said to them both. I opened my blanket and looked down at my body. After eight months in a cast, I was just skin and bones.

"Wiggle your toes," Rawling said gently.

I was scared. What if only my toes worked? I wiggled them. They moved. But I wasn't surprised at that. They'd moved when I was in the body cast. Without waiting for instruction from Rawling, I tried to swing my legs at the knees.

I felt stabs of pain. Water filled my eyes. But not from the pain.

"Did you see that!" I almost yelled.

"It wasn't a breeze, was it," Rawling answered. "Your feet actually swung a little."

"Yes," I said. I did it again. They moved only a fraction of an inch, but they moved. *My legs worked!*

Rawling cleared his throat a couple of times and looked at my dad.

I saw my dad swallow hard, as if he were trying to say something. Then I realized he, too, was fighting tears.

"I think," Rawling said, his voice shaky, "that the operation was successful. But that doesn't mean you can walk. Yet. Build up the muscles with exercise and go slow. Then you can learn to walk."

You can walk.

What a sweet, sweet phrase. After a lifetime in a wheelchair. I could hardly believe it.

I turned to Dad with a big smile.

Dad's face, however, was troubled.

"Dad?" I said quietly, not understanding his reaction to the news that I could walk. Really walk! Didn't he want me to be able to walk?

Or was it that something else was bothering him?

"Tyce, I'm so . . . happy for you . . . for all of us. What great news!" he exclaimed finally. "I wish I could wait and let us all celebrate a while longer," he said slowly and sadly. "But I just found out that we've lost all communication with Earth. The tekkie guys came and told me since they couldn't find you."

"All communication? Impossible." This came from Rawling.

"They said the dome's mainframe computer is malfunctioning," Dad answered.

"The hard drive can't be down," Rawling argued. "The

rest of the dome is running fine. And we've got two backup mainframes."

"Rawling," Dad answered patiently, "all I know is what the computer tekkies told me. Some virus has wiped out all the software in the communications segment of the hard drive. We can't reach Earth. Earth can't reach us."

"We've got backup software. They can reinstall it," Rawling insisted.

Dad shook his head. "It has disappeared. And with no link to Earth, there's no way to download another copy."

The room went silent as we all thought about what that meant.

Rawling closed his eyes. "No communication with Earth. The Manchurian fleet approaches. How much worse can this get?"

Dad coughed.

Rawling opened his eyes and stared at him. "You're telling me this *can* get worse?"

"The surface-to-space missile system that arrived with us. We haven't had time to put it in place, of course. But I don't know if it will do any good. All the trigger devices are gone."

"Gone? Impossible. We've had that equipment securely locked down. And under video surveillance."

"That's just it, Rawling. While you've been in here with Tyce, I asked to review the videotapes from the minute the equipment was being unloaded up until now. No one has been near it here on Mars. It looks like the trigger devices were missing before I even brought the stuff down on the shuttle. But how could that be? Our last message from Earth confirmed that the trigger devices had been sent with the equipment."

"So you're telling me the impossible." Rawling rubbed

his face. "Someone stole them in the six months of travel between Earth and Mars. In outer space. On an unmanned ship."

Dad nodded. "That's about it. And now we've got a hostile Manchurian space fleet approaching, no communication with Earth, and no weapons to protect us." He gave me a weak smile. "But at least Tyce should be able to walk soon."

I'm not sure it was much of a consolation if Mars was going to be invaded.

CHAPTER 13

Butterscotch sky. Blue sun edging over the outline of distant mountains. It was still morning, so wisps of blue cloud still appeared in the sky. They'd disappear when the day became warmer.

There was no oxygen, and a wind of 80 miles an hour rattled sand against the titanium of our robots. It was minus 100 degrees Fahrenheit.

That's what it was like outside of the Mars Dome as I rolled my robot body across the packed red soil with Ashley's robot beside it.

It was around 11 o'clock. Only an hour had passed since Dad had shared his grim news.

On the inside of the dome, Ashley and I were hooked to the computers. As were all the other kids who controlled robots. They had sent their robots to the first carbon-dioxide generator site, a half mile away from the dome. This had been the first equipment unloaded by shuttle from the unmanned spaceships above us in orbit.

The harsh Martian environment was the reason for the robots. Robots could work outside far more easily and faster than humans in space suits. There was far less danger too. A hole in a space suit could mean death for a human. In fact, without the strength of the titanium robots and their ability to work outside, it would have been nearly impossible to assemble the generators. Engineers calculated it would have otherwise taken thousands of human workers, and the dome couldn't sustain all those people.

"I hope we find something that will help Rawling," Ashley's robot said to mine. We were hooked up by wireless audio. "Everyone is pretty nervous about the Manchurian space fleet."

"Maybe not everyone," I answered. Ashley and I were directing our robots to the repaired puncture of the dome, while all the other robots went to the work site to unpack the crates that held the equipment. "Perhaps someone is helping them from this end."

That was the reason for the communications breakdown. As we had found out this afternoon, someone under the dome had introduced the virus to wipe out the communications software on the mainframe. And that same person had stolen the backup disks. The same person who had found a way to get outside the dome and somehow put a small hole in it? But who? There were 200 scientists and tekkies, plus another 50 robot-control kids.

We rolled our robots around the outer edge of the dome. The dome itself was about the size of four football fields.

"Here it is," I said, pointing at the patch.

The dome towered high above our robots, gleaming black in the weak sunlight.

"Another thing I don't get," Ashley said, "is why. If Rawling is right and someone somehow got out of the dome to do this, what would it gain him or her? I mean, the emergency patch was in place in less than five minutes. And why try to harm the dome if you have to live in it too?"

I didn't have an answer, so I couldn't give her one. Instead I searched the ground with the visual signals sent to my brain through the robot's video lenses.

All I saw were footsteps. Dozens and dozens. Which made sense. This was where the repair crew had spent hours putting the permanent patch in place. If one person had once stood here and done something at head height to cause the hole, his or her footprints were long destroyed.

"Where are you going?" Ashley asked as I directed my robot to begin rolling away from the dome.

"Just wondering if I can see anything better from a distance," I answered. "I—"

"You what?"

"Come here!"

Ashley's robot rolled to meet mine. We were less than 20 human steps away from the wall of the dome.

"Look at these tracks," I said.

"Tire tracks. It's where the platform buggy stopped. And here's where everyone climbed down."

"Yes," I said. "But what about those footprints there?"

My robot arm pointed away from the dome at a single set of footprints. "See? The footprints end at the edge of the platform buggy tire tracks. That means the footprints were there first. And the tire tracks ran them over after. And there's something else."

"The footprints are walking *toward* the dome."

"Exactly," I told Ashley. "And it's the only set of footprints. So where did this person come from?"

"That should be easy to answer. We just track the footprints backward."

We found the answer two miles away. Over a hill. Hidden from the dome.

And when we found the answer, we didn't bother wasting any time. We disconnected immediately, leaving the robots near what we had found.

Back in the computer lab, we took off our helmets and helped each other disconnect.

Ashley helped me into my wheelchair since my legs were still so weak. Usually I insisted on pushing myself. Not this time.

She raced my wheelchair forward, from the computer lab toward Rawling's office.

We had to talk to him as soon as possible.

CHAPTER 14

Forty-five minutes later Mom, Dad, and Rawling stood behind my wheelchair in Rawling's office. Ashley sat beside me. The lights were dim, and a large television screen was flickering.

"Ready?" Rawling asked.

He must have taken our silence as a yes since he hit a button on his remote. The television screen darkened briefly. Then it showed the eerie reds and oranges of the Martian landscape.

I knew what we would see. This visual input had just been recorded through my robot's computer. Because the robot was on wheels, it was a steady image. It showed the footprints that Ashley and I had followed. It showed the hill we had first climbed and then descended. And, on the other side, hidden beneath an outcropping, it showed what we had found.

A small shuttle ship.

Dad whistled. "That's a two-person ship. Mainly used on the Moon to take people up to orbiting spaceships."

Next the visual lurched a little. My robot had rolled into a small depression as I brought it in for a closer look. Then the visual zoomed in close on a symbol on the side of the shuttle.

"Manchurian!" Mom exclaimed. "That's the shape of a Manchurian flag."

The image on the television suddenly went dark. That was the point where Ashley and I had decided to disengage from our robots and find Rawling immediately.

Rawling moved to the wall of his office and hit the light switch. "As you know," he said, pacing the floor, "Ashley and Tyce found this with their robots an hour ago. Unless we are reading this totally wrong, it looks like someone landed in the shuttle—"

"But from where?" Dad interrupted. "Something that small can't travel more than 1,000 miles. It doesn't hold the oxygen and food needed to travel here from Earth or the Moon."

"I can't guess where at this point," Rawling answered. "For now, let's just stick with what we know from the evidence."

"The footprints led away from the abandoned shuttle toward the dome," Mom said.

"More specifically, toward the point of puncture of the dome," Rawling added. "We can guess that the person used some device, maybe an explosive, to punch the hole through about head height. But why? And then what?"

I had a mental image of a man with a space suit walking into the tunnel of the dome. And then the answer hit me.

"To create a diversion," I said. "Earlier we couldn't figure out why someone would make a puncture that was so easy to repair. Because it only made for temporary confusion. And it also guaranteed that the main entrance to the dome would be opened for that person as the repair crews went out."

I told them about the person in the space suit. "That

must have been the space-shuttle pilot. All he or she had to do was get inside, never to be noticed with all the new people and new activity. There are plenty of places to hide if no one is looking for you."

"And I'll bet once he got inside," Rawling said, speaking slowly as he thought aloud, "the next thing he did was disable the communications system."

Mom gripped my shoulder. "I don't suppose you had your robot's visual on record when you approached this person."

"No," I said. "I was just trying to get some freedom. Then the—"

I was almost about to say "headache hit me." But so far I'd only told Rawling. This definitely wasn't the time to burden Mom and Dad with something so minor, compared to the crisis of the dome.

"Then the . . . ?" Mom prompted.

Then came a horrible thought. "Dad, remember in space when you told me the Manchurians would never destroy the dome itself?"

He nodded. "I said the fleet would never fire any weapons on the dome. That they would want to be able to land and send in soldiers because it was important they get Mars with the dome and the generators intact."

"And you said you couldn't figure out why the fleet would follow us, knowing we have the surface-to-space atomic weapons to protect us."

"The triggers!" Ashley said. "Stolen. Now the missiles won't work. Do you think . . ."

Suddenly all the pieces of the puzzle snapped together in my brain. "I think I can guess why the fleet is on its way," I said. "They've sent someone ahead. One person. And he was to be inside the dome. Preparing it for the arrival of the fleet."

CHAPTER 15

"Ugly," Ashley said at 3:30 that afternoon.

"Hey," I protested. She had just arrived at my mini-dome, where I had been waiting for her after eating a quick lunch. "This is me you're talking about."

In my lap was a blanket, a pair of binoculars, and a stuffed pillowcase. Sewn onto the pillowcase were two arms made of tubes of cloth filled with rags. Mom had helped me sew a crude head, made of a smaller stuffed pillowcase, on top.

I held it up for more inspection. "For half a body, it might just work as a decoy. Think the guy in the space suit will think it's me?"

"Let's hope so. You ready?"

I jammed the half-body back on top of the binoculars in my lap. I covered it with a blanket.

"Ready," I said. "Take me to the top."

⚛

Ashley wheeled me to the observatory on the third-level deck of the dome. It was a short trip. After all, the total area of the dome was only about four of Earth's football fields.

The main level of the dome held the mini-domes and labs. One level up, a walkway about 10 feet wide circled the inside of the dome walls. The third level, centered at the top of the dome, could be reached only by a narrow catwalk from the second level.

The floor of it was a circle only 15 feet wide. It hung directly below the ceiling, above the exact middle of the main level. Here a powerful telescope perched beneath a round bubble of clear, thick glass that stuck up from the black glass that made up the rest of the dome. From there, the massive telescope gave an incredible view of the solar system.

It was my favorite place in the dome. I'd spent a lot of hours there—observing the stars, asteroids, and planets. And also asking "why" questions about God and the universe. Every time I was up here, I marveled again at how God had created everything—all the "matter"—and then made it work together, in some kind of perfect harmony that scientists could find no natural explanation for. It had been through all my hours spent in the observatory, as well as all the crises I'd faced on Mars before going to Earth, that I'd come to believe that I had a soul—a part of me invisible to science and medicine. A part of me that feels love, happiness, hope, and sadness. A part of me that knows God loves us and yet still wonders why God can allow bad things to happen to us . . . like the pending Manchurian invasion.

But now wasn't the time for deep thoughts.

Ashley parked the wheelchair in front of the telescope eyepieces. I set the brakes and lifted the blanket off of me. I gave Ashley the binoculars, which she set on the floor.

"This is the tricky part," I said, lifting the half-body out of my lap. "Can you prop this behind my back?"

I leaned forward. She quickly shoved the stuffed pillowcases between my back and the wheelchair, making sure the fake head was right behind my own head.

"Now the arms," I said.

As we had planned beforehand, Ashley lifted the half-body's arms to the telescope controls. She taped them in place, its arms wrapped around my face, to make sure we had the height and angle right—so the dummy would look like a real person. We wanted it at the telescope so I could look down on the dome from a more hidden position.

With the dummy in position, Ashley held my arms and helped lower me beneath the dummy's arms as I wiggled feet forward out of the wheelchair. It was strange to actually feel the floor of the observatory against my legs. Even though my muscles were weak, I was able to roll over onto my belly.

I glanced upward at the wheelchair.

Ashley was already moving the dummy's head forward against the eyepieces. She taped it in place too. "What do you think?" she asked.

"People hardly ever think to look up here anytime," I said, "so we're probably safe 'til nightfall." Right now it was 3:30 in the afternoon. The weak sunlight was already fading. It couldn't penetrate the black superglass of the dome. "And if anyone does look up here, it's dim enough that I think the outline will fool anyone into thinking I'm still in my wheelchair. Just to be sure, take a look once you get down, and call me on the wrist buzzer."

Ashley knelt beside me. She had carried two wrist buzzers—small communicating devices that looked just like watches. She gave me one and kept the other.

"See you in a while," she said. "I'll come back later as

planned to help you back into your wheelchair. In the meantime, if you need anything, just buzz me."

"Thanks."

As she left, I crawled to the edge of the observatory floor with my binoculars beside me.

Two minutes later the wrist buzzer crackled.

"Fooled me," Ashley said. "And I knew what to look for."

"Good," I answered.

Now I was ready to watch as long as it took to spot the intruder. Even better, I'd have a surprise waiting!

CHAPTER 16

I surveyed the area below.

I could see the mini-domes, the small, dark, plastic huts where each scientist and tekkie lives in privacy from the others. And then there were the experimental labs and open areas, where equipment was maintained. Some people were using the second-level walkway for exercise, jogging in circles above the main floor below.

The dome now held the original 200 people, plus the other 50 who had arrived with the space fleet. In terms of living space, it was a lot more crowded. But as soon as the carbon-dioxide generators were built, expansion of the dome would be next. In the meantime, three research areas had been temporarily shut down.

In the first research area, a mini-dome had been erected as a huge dorm area for all 50 robot-control kids.

And the last two research areas had been converted to a computer area, holding cots and transmitters for all the kids when they were using their robot-control capabilities to work on the generators. According to strict instructions from the World United Federation, the kids were only allowed to control the robots in shifts of four hours a day.

Then they were free to follow up on schoolwork and have playtime.

Right now, many of the kids were hooked up. As they lay on cots, each wore a helmet to block out the sights and sounds of the dome. Each was busy controlling a robot that was working at the carbon-dioxide generator site.

This time it wasn't any of the kids I was worried about. No, I was watching for an adult who was doing something unusual.

More specifically—although I hadn't told anyone because it seemed too dumb—I was watching for the one person I knew who had enough computer skills to hack his way into the mainframe computer. It was something he had done before. And even though I couldn't believe he had somehow returned, my gut told me he had to be the one responsible.

I had learned the hard way. Of anyone in the Terrataker terrorist group that served the Manchurians, he was the genius who didn't care how many people died for him to get his way.

His name was Luke Daab. He'd masqueraded as a maintenance engineer—a sort of janitor—on the *Moon Racer.* After planning to crash the spaceship into the sun, he'd escaped into one of the pods. He'd last been reported hiding out in the Manchurian Sector of the Moon, a place that gave him diplomatic immunity from the World United Federation Military. Now, impossible as it seemed, I wouldn't be surprised if I saw him in my binoculars.

So as the minutes ticked by, I scanned the floor below. Stray thoughts hit me. My stomach began to growl.

Ashley had been right to accuse me earlier of filling my head with things because I was in a body cast and had little else to do.

Only now I was glad about it. Because—despite Rawling's quick check that didn't show a tumor—if there was seriously something in my brain that was causing these headaches, at least I knew that dying wouldn't be the worst thing to happen to me.

Some people say that science points us away from God, but I've learned that isn't true. The more and more I've learned about science—and the creation of the universe—the easier it is to believe that God is behind it.

On this space trip, I'd been reading a lot more about astronomy. And I was discovering that some astronomers believed that science clearly showed God had made this universe.

Like this weird detail, for instance. Physics show that in the beginning moments of the universe, energy produced matter and antimatter. It might sound like comic-book stuff, but when particles of matter and particles of antimatter touch, both are destroyed. Physicists say that what should have happened is that all matter should have been exploded by antimatter. No matter should have survived anywhere. In fact, this universe should have become merely space with a weak radiation below the energy of a single microwave oven.

Instead—for no reason anyone in science can explain—for every 10 billion bits of antimatter, 10 billion and one bits of matter were created. The stuff left over—one bit for every 10 billion—was enough to make everything in the universe.

One mathematician figured out the chances that the universe would grow in such a way to support life. It was less than one in 10^{123}. That's a 10 followed by 123 zeros.

Somehow, against the odds of $\frac{1}{10}^{123}$, the universe grew in such a way to make life possible on Earth.

Is it so crazy for anyone to wonder if God was behind all of this?

It was now 5:30 in the afternoon. I had fought a headache for 10 minutes, grateful it wasn't so bad that I had to scream. That would have ruined my cover in a fairly small dome for sure.

When it passed, something strange caught my eye. A man was at the far wall of the dome. Away from the main traffic area. He was struggling to roll a huge cylindrical tank off a wagon.

It was dim there, and I could only see an outline of a figure.

Luke Daab! It had to be! The figure was skinny and short, just like him. And Luke had this weird hunched over way of walking, just like this guy.

But even more, I could see no reason for the tank to be placed there.

As I watched, the man hurried away with the wagon. A minute later he returned with another equally large tank. He looked around in all directions, as if making sure he was unseen. He rolled off the second tank, then hurried away.

Explosives? Getting them ready to detonate when the Manchurian fleet arrived? After all, if everyone in here were dead, the Manchurian soldiers wouldn't have to fight anyone.

I brought my wrist buzzer to my mouth as the small figure returned with a third container.

"Ashley!" I hissed into the wrist buzzer.

Seconds later, she replied, "Tyce!"

"Get Rawling," I said. I hadn't moved the binoculars from my eyes. The man was returning with a fourth tank.

"Quick! Get Rawling or Dad and anyone else who can help on short notice and go to the south end of the dome. Grab the guy who's unloading some big cylinders. I haven't seen anything like them under the dome before. They could be explosives!"

CHAPTER 17

"Compressed oxygen," Rawling said an hour later.

I was back in my wheelchair, back in his office. It was 6:30—almost time for dinner. Ashley had helped me down from the upper deck, then gone to get something to eat herself.

Rawling waved some papers. "Here's the work order from the chief engineer. They're going to run some ventilation pipes around the inner wall of the dome. Then they're going to hook up those oxygen tanks to the pipes. Now that we've increased the dome's population, it's a backup system for the emergency oxygen tubes. If there's any threat to the dome's atmosphere, those big tanks of compressed oxygen will automatically release."

"Chief engineer's idea?"

"Straight from Earth." Rawling grimaced. "*Before* the communications virus. All of the equipment was on one of the unmanned spaceships."

"What did he say about the guy unloading it?" I asked.

"He asked one of the tekkies to do it. I checked. You really think Luke is back?" he asked with raised eyebrows.

Then he continued, "The tekkie *is* about the same size as Luke."

Rawling, too, knew what Luke Daab looked like. Daab had been a maintenance tekkie on Mars since the beginning of the Project. Invisible as he worked, his job gave him access to absolutely everything under the dome. And that kind of access had served well—especially on the *Moon Racer,* the spaceship Ashley, Dad, and I had taken back to Earth to find and rescue the other robot-control kids. Because we'd never suspected he might be a Terrataker, we were almost killed.

"Someone came in on that two-person shuttle. It wouldn't surprise me if . . ." I stopped. "If that shuttle had been attached to one of the unmanned spaceships. It could happen, right? That near the Moon as the fleet is assembled, a Manchurian ship delivers Luke and the two-person shuttle to one of our unmanned ships. And they hitchhike across the solar system."

"The Manchurians do have the resources and technology to do that," Rawling said. Still, there was doubt in his voice. "But even if Luke got inside the unmanned ship—"

"That part would be easy. A hatch. He'd—"

"He'd still need oxygen and supplies for all those months of travel."

"Unloaded from the same Manchurian ship that brought him there."

"Maybe," Rawling said. "I'll send someone up in our own shuttle to take a close look at the unmanned vehicles in orbit. In the meantime, I'm thinking of stopping all work, assembling everybody in one area of the dome, and doing a thorough search for whoever it is who sneaked in."

"It would be to our advantage," I argued, "if that person didn't know we knew about him. I can spend more time up in the observatory looking for him, right? We've still got at least two months before the Manchurian fleet gets here."

"That dummy up there at the telescope does look pretty convincing from down below," Rawling said. He grinned. "Much as we miss your help with the carbon-dioxide generators, maybe I can afford to give you a little more time. But try not to get too excited tonight when you see tekkies sealing off the temporary dome for the other kids."

"Sealing?"

"Part of that emergency backup plan. The World United Federation has literally invested billions in robot control. The future of Mars colonization depends on those 50 kids. So their sleeping area is being sealed. If anything happens to the pressure or oxygen level of the dome, at least they'll be safe until the problem is fixed."

"The adults can die first, huh," I said, making a bad joke.

"Let's face it," Rawling said. "Everything now depends on those who can control robots. Which includes you. So if you happen to see Luke Daab, don't go running after him. Got it?"

"That would be great, though," I said. "Being able to run. And finally stopping Luke Daab."

Rawling groaned. "I never should have put that idea in your head. Get some sleep tonight. And go back up to the telescope tomorrow."

"First I'm going to the exercise room," I told Rawling. "You have no idea how badly I want to get these legs ready to walk."

Rawling smiled. "Maybe not. But I can guess. Go exercise. Then sleep. It will help your body."

Sleep. That would be good. But I knew I wouldn't sleep

much. The headaches would hit me like clockwork, just like every night since leaving Earth.

And the next one, I guessed, would be on me in less than three hours.

CHAPTER 18

From Rawling's office, I wheeled toward the exercise area to spend time with the weights. Even in the reduced gravity of Mars, Rawling had said I'd only be able to move five-pound weights a total of one inch with the leg machine.

But for me, that was incredible.

My legs were responding to my brain's commands. In that aspect, the operation had been successful. Now I needed to add muscle to legs that had never had muscle before. And then—I finally dared hope for it—I could teach those legs to walk.

If it weren't for my killer headaches and the approach of the Manchurian fleet, I would have been bouncing around for joy 24 hours a day.

For now, I was only going to approach everything one day at a time, knowing the Manchurians wouldn't be here for a while.

And that included my weight program.

Just as I rounded the corner to the exercise area, someone in a regular jumpsuit uniform stepped out. I barely glimpsed his face as he walked away and told myself it were just my imagination.

That was not Luke Daab. As if I were going to go running to Rawling again. But maybe someone in the exercise area could tell me who it was.

Except it was empty when I rolled into it.

I headed straight to the leg machine. On it was taped an envelope with my name. I opened it, puzzled.

Tyce, those headaches can kill you if you don't take it easy and stop looking for me. You haven't felt the worst of it yet. Expect a sample of how bad it can get within the next minute.

In the next minute?

Someone was controlling my headaches?

Then I realized something. The man who had just stepped out of the exercise area had been in a standard blue jumpsuit. Not exercise gear. Why else had he been here, except to leave this note?

But how had he known I would be coming here right now?

And how was he controlling the head—

I heard a scream. Dimly knew it was mine. I fell out of my wheelchair, flailing my arms at the pain. This headache was much worse than anything I'd felt before.

Even death would be better than this agony, a part of my mind thought.

The pain continued and continued until it hurt so bad I couldn't even scream.

I waited for a blackout to give me mercy, but it didn't come.

And finally, when the headache stopped pinching my

brain, I gasped for breath. My body was shaking and sweating.

I had to find that person. If only to beg him never to do that to me again.

CHAPTER 19

"Tyce?"

The voice came from outside the doorway of my bedroom. I was just about to roll out of my wheelchair and get into bed. After that headache attack, there was no way I could exercise. Half an hour had passed before I could even get back to our mini-dome. Now, an hour later, I was still trembling, and I'd thrown up twice from the aftereffects of the pain.

It was now 8:30 P.M. Mom and Dad had been so concerned about me that they'd gone to get Rawling.

"Yes, Rawling," I said. My voice was a croak. "Come in."

He did, carrying the lead-wrapped belt that he'd used to shield me during the X-ray process.

"Great," I groaned. "More medical work. Got some needles for painkillers? Those pills you gave me haven't done a thing."

"I think I know why."

I glanced at my watch. "Speak quickly," I said. "If it follows the schedule, the next headache is due in less than a minute."

That was the worst of it. Knowing and anticipating when

the headaches would arrive. Like getting up in the morning and knowing you had a dentist appointment. Except this was like three or four dentist appointments a day. Without the freezing.

"I thought it was strange that there were no medical notes about the implant in your spine," Rawling said. "So I went to your father this afternoon just before he took the shuttle up. The communications link between Mars and Earth might be down, but he still has his Terrataker database."

I knew exactly what Rawling meant. I'd been surprised to find out on Earth that my dad had been working against the Terratakers for years. He and Rawling were special agents who'd trained together in New York, even before the Mars Project was launched. And Dad had a list of every person with a known or suspected link to the Terratakers.

"Sure enough," Rawling said. "Far, far down the list, I spotted the name of one of the doctors on your medical team. His background shows him listed as a potential supporter of the Terratakers."

"But why would a Terrataker be allowed to—"

"The Terratakers have plenty of spies and connections in the World United Federation. I imagine that someone somewhere pulled a string."

"Rawling, the operation was successful."

"More successful than you think. I scanned your spinal X ray into the computer and zoomed in. That implant—"

I interrupted him with a low scream. The headache had arrived. I clenched my teeth against the pain and made no more noise.

"Tyce! Is it always this bad?"

I groaned.

"You should have told someone earlier."

I groaned again.

Rawling rushed forward with the lead belt. He wrapped it around my belly, then slid it down so that it rested on my hips.

And the pain stopped!

"That better?" Rawling asked.

I found myself panting with relief.

"Thought so."

"What is it?" I asked, amazed at the peace and calm I felt.

"The implant has tiny, tiny pincers. The nerves to your spinal column have grown in and around the pincers. I think someone is squeezing those nerves whenever they want to put you in agony. Spinal nerves are funny. Even though they're pinched in your back, the pain can be anywhere in your body."

"And the lead belt?" I queried. "Not that I'm complaining . . ."

"Shields you from whatever signals that person is using to activate the implant from a remote source."

I lifted the belt slightly. The pain returned in full force.

I lowered the belt. The pain stopped.

"Rawling." I was still panting. "It's the kind of relief that comes when someone finally quits hitting your thumb with a hammer."

"You'll get some sleep?"

"Yes!"

"Good. In the morning, come talk to me."

He left. Or at least I think he did.

I was so exhausted from fighting the pain that I was asleep before he could shut the door on his way out.

CHAPTER 20

A dream woke me. When I rubbed my eyes, the thought was still there.

Hunt the hunter.

I was still half asleep.

Hunt the hunter.

Why was I having that thought? Was my subconscious trying to tell me something? I tried to recall the details of the dream. . . .

I was swimming in the ocean. Luke Daab cast a lure from his fishing rod. He hooked me below the spine and began to reel me in. Except in my dream I grew bigger and stronger and turned into a half shark. Instead of letting Luke Daab reel me in like a helpless fish, I turned and swam hard. He was pulled into the water, and I turned around and opened my big shark mouth and was just about to chomp on his head—

Weird dream. I remembered I had woken up just as Luke screamed. With the same scream of pain that this implant had given me time after time over the last months.

I rubbed my eyes more.

Hunt the hunter.

I thought more about the dream. I realized that Luke had used the fishing rod to reel me in, but in the end, it became the weapon used on him.

Hunt the hunter.

When I realized what that meant, I tried to sit bolt upright.

It didn't work. I was still too weak, especially with the weight of the lead belt around my waist. I was only able to roll over and look at the clock. Eleven-thirty at night. I'd slept nearly three hours straight, my longest stretch in months.

Hunt the hunter. Turn his weapon against him.

I was about to call out to Dad, in our shared living area, but then I remembered. Dad had just left in the shuttle to pick up the rest of the cargo. Mom was most likely still in the lab.

But there was still plenty of time to find Rawling. He always tended to work late so, with luck, he'd still be in his office.

"Rawling!" I called out frantically.

It had been a struggle to get into my jumpsuit by myself, but at least with all the weight I'd lost in the body cast, my clothing was so loose it easily fit over the lead belt.

Rawling looked up from his desk as I rolled in. He had been writing on a pad of paper. "I expected you to sleep through the night," he said, one eyebrow raised.

"I think I know how to find him," I answered. "Use his weapon against him."

"Slow down. Him?"

"The person we think broke into the dome. The person I think is Luke Daab. Who put a virus in the computer software. Who stole the triggers we need to launch our defense system against the Manchurian invasion. That him. Let's use his weapon against him."

Rawling gave me a smile. "Again. Slow down. His weapon?"

"Whatever device he's been using to activate the implant in my spinal column."

Rawling set his pen down. "How do you know it's the same person?"

"I've had those headaches all through the journey here," I explained quickly.

Rawling scratched his head, looking dubious.

"Remote activation technology is great," I continued, trying to follow my own reasoning, "but the most range I've heard of is 10,000 miles. It couldn't be someone from Earth, then, or someone from Mars. It had to be someone traveling with the fleet. But everyone who was part of the fleet was cleared by security checks. So it has to be the one person who hitchhiked along and landed his own space shuttle. That person didn't go through security clearance, I can guarantee you that."

An image flashed through my mind. Of my robot going up to the man in the space suit. Of the man pulling his arm out of his space-suit sleeve.

"And, Rawling," I finished, "when this guy entered the dome, he reached inside his space suit. It had to be for the remote. He wanted a headache to shut me and my robot control down. That tells me he's very familiar with the situation around here."

Rawling spun around in his chair a few times. It was a habit he had when he was thinking. I'd learned not to interrupt.

"I'll give you this," he said slowly. "Your hitchhiker theory was right. Your dad just radioed me from orbit. The unmanned spaceship that was carrying the surface-to-space missile system has marks on the outer hull where a space shuttle docked. And a close inspection of the interior showed that someone had been living in it. Which explains how the triggers to the missile system were stolen before they even reached Mars."

"So you'll agree it's possible the same person was zapping the implant in my spinal cord."

"Say I do agree . . . ," he began.

"Then we track him," I said quickly, "by scanning for whatever wave technology his remote uses. I'm guessing X-ray. That's what we use for robot control. Find the frequency that triggers my implant, and then we can follow the same frequency right to its source. He'll never know we're looking for him, right up to the second we get him."

Rawling spun in his chair some more. After a few minutes he stared at me, his jaw set. "It's going to hurt you."

"So will a Manchurian fleet that lands when we don't have missiles to scare them away."

"We'll do it then," Rawling said.

"No, you won't." It was a voice behind us.

I turned just in time to see a face I recognized.

Luke Daab's.

He held a neuron gun pointed at Rawling's head. If set on stun, the voltage of just one neuron gun could cripple him with the pain of an electrical jolt through the nerve pathways of his body. Although it didn't do permanent damage, it would temporarily paralyze his muscles and render him unconscious. But if on a different setting . . . I'd never seen those results, and I didn't want to.

Without warning, Daab pulled the trigger.

Rawling screamed briefly, then fell straight back over his

chair. He twitched once on the floor, then made no movement at all.

"Hello, Tyce," Luke said with a sinister smile. "So glad we could finally get together again."

CHAPTER 21

Luke Daab shut the door to Rawling's office and locked it. Keeping the neuron gun trained at my head, he moved to Rawling's desk and ripped the computer wires loose. He did the same with the phone line.

I was trapped—with one of the most evil Terrataker masterminds in the universe.

"Just in case you had thoughts of trying to reach anyone when I left," Daab said casually. "I have no intention of letting you stop me ever again."

He was still as redheaded, mousy, and skinny as ever. The only change seemed to be that his beach-ball belly was a bit larger.

I couldn't speak. Was Rawling unconscious . . . or dead?

"Cat got your tongue?" Daab asked with a slight, twisted smile and that nervous laugh of his. He yanked off my wrist buzzer and then pulled a small device from his pocket. He dangled the device just out of my reach. "Or is it a headache?"

I groaned. I didn't want him to realize that the lead wrap was shielding me from his remote.

"Why?" I said between clenched teeth. Although I didn't have a headache, I still felt enough anguish that I didn't have to act out any pain.

Luke moved around behind my wheelchair. He spoke to my back. "Why the implant? Or why am I here?"

My world tilted. He had lifted the handles of my wheelchair. He gave a violent jerk, and I tumbled helplessly forward. My elbows crashed into the floor. I groaned again and slowly rolled over.

Daab sat in my wheelchair, smiling down on me. "I'm here in this office because you and Rawling have suddenly become a danger. This is a little earlier than I had planned to set everything in motion, but fortunately all the pieces are in place."

I said nothing.

"Why am I here on Mars?" he asked. "Oh, you've already figured that out. To get the dome ready for my friends. You're going to be a big help to me, Tyce. I've always known you were smart, but listening in on your conversations with Rawling confirmed it for me."

His catlike smile widened. "Oh yes, the first thing I did once I got inside was plant a simple bug under Rawling's desk. I did want to know what was happening. It was great entertainment, listening to how you came to your conclusions. I was amazed at how accurate they were. That only proves it was a good choice to enlist you for our side."

"Never help," I said between clenched teeth. I tried to rise.

Daab stood from the wheelchair and kicked me back onto the floor. I was surprised at how strong a skinny guy like him could be.

As he turned around, I quickly shifted the lead belt, lifting it slightly upward. I couldn't depend on him announcing when he shut off the pain activator. I didn't want him to find out I had a shield, or he'd take away my only protection.

Immediately pain flooded my head. This time my groan of agony was real.

Daab sat back in the wheelchair, smiled, and dangled the remote again. "So far, on a scale of 1 to 10, I've kept this down to a four. Today in the exercise room, I raised it to a six. There's still a lot higher pain ahead for you. Unless you cooperate." He hit the remote. "Feel better now?"

The pain stopped. I let out a big sigh of relief.

"Perhaps you can concentrate now," Daab said. "So listen closely. Very soon, the only people living under the dome will be you, me, and all the other kids with robot-control capabilities. I know you are considered their leader. And you're going to make sure they continue assembling the generators so that everything is ready by the time Dr. Jordan and my other Terrataker and Manchurian friends arrive. If you don't help, the headaches will return—and you'll wish you were dead."

I remembered how bad it was in the exercise room, thinking that I would have begged to have the pain end.

"The fleet is two months away," I said. "I can't keep 50 kids from finding a way to stop you."

"I won't be in the dome." He sneered. "I'll be orbiting safely in space while I monitor the progress of the generator assembly. That's why you'll be in charge. And if you don't help, I'll shuttle back down once a week to execute kids until they finally get the message I'm serious."

Daab looked at his watch, as if it weren't a big deal to talk about killing people in cold blood. "11:45 P.M. Good, all the robot-control kids should now be asleep in their nice little airtight, oxygen-filled dorm. When they wake up, they'll have the whole planet to themselves. Except, of course, for you and me."

Daab stood again, moved to the wall, and took down one of the two emergency oxygen tubes from beside a fire extinguisher. He dropped it on the floor in front of my face. "Ten minutes, give or take," he said. "Then it will do you a lot of good to wear this until the oxygen runs out."

He moved back to the wall and grabbed the other oxygen tube for himself. "I guess from your point of view it's a shame that Rawling didn't pay closer attention to those huge tanks labeled oxygen. You know, the ones that you thought were explosive devices?"

Daab kicked Rawling, who had not yet moved. Then Daab made himself comfortable again in my wheelchair. "I can give you the whole story later, of course, but here's the short of it. As you know, the upper levels of the World United Federation are riddled with Manchurian supporters. So it was very simple for them to arrange the emergency backup system. Seal the dorm. Add those oxygen tanks. No one questioned it. Only the tanks don't have oxygen. They hold a highly poisonous gas. The robot-control kids are safe, but all the adults will be dead as soon as I hook the tanks up to the ventilation system."

He glanced one more time at his watch. "Like I said, 10 minutes. Just before midnight. Make sure your oxygen mask is on. I'll have all the adults dead and the poisonous gas cleared before your supply runs out."

He began to roll the chair around me. "Nearly forgot." He looked down at me and giggled. "Can't leave you there on the floor to stop me now, can I?"

I didn't see his fingers activate the controls on the remote, but again a grenade went off in my brain. I screamed.

"That's a seven," he said harshly. "Enjoy it. I'll end your pain when I've released the gas. That will be your warning to put on your oxygen mask."

With that, he rolled to the door in my wheelchair, opened the door without rising, and cackled as he scooted out of Rawling's office.

CHAPTER 22

Ten minutes.

I could hardly move my arms, the pain was so intense. My fingers shook as I grabbed that lead belt. Twice my hands lost their grip. The third time, I managed to push it down and the shield blocked the transmission from the remote.

My head filled with blessed silence.

Ten minutes, I thought in agony.

I crawled to Rawling, dragging my oxygen tube. If he was alive, he was helpless, unable to protect himself.

I put my ear up to his mouth and heard breathing. I slipped the oxygen mask over his head and activated the tube. All of this had probably taken 30 seconds.

Now what?

Hunt the hunter.

The words of my dream came back with crystal clarity. Words that might save not only my life, but everyone's under the dome.

I was on the floor, close to the desk. Reaching up, I grabbed the edge of the desk and pulled myself off the floor. Leaning against the desk, I could stand.

Any other time, I would have shouted with joy. My legs, weak as they were, much as I needed the desk, still supported me! It truly was a miracle!

I shuffled around the desk to the closest wall. Keeping one hand on the desk, I reached to the wall with my other hand and pulled down a large, framed print of a sunset on Earth. I smashed the middle of it against the corner edge of the desk. Glass shattered. Now I had an empty frame.

Nine minutes.

I turned the frame on its side. The top of the frame was now waist-high to me. With the bottom of it against the floor, I held it beside me and leaned on it.

Then I took the first baby step of my life.

This was no time to celebrate. I was wobbly and felt like I would fall any second. But if I did, how could I get up without crawling back to the desk? And that would waste too many precious seconds.

The phrase of the dream came back to me again, making me feel stronger: *Hunt the hunter.*

I took the second baby step of my life. And the third. I tottered forward to the office door.

I was desperately hoping one thing. That Luke Daab had not risked raising any questions by being seen in my wheelchair. That he had jumped out almost as soon as he'd left the office.

I opened the door and peeked around the corner.

There it was. My wheelchair. I exhaled with relief.

I wanted to drop the heavy lead belt to be able to walk faster. But if I did, the headache pain would paralyze me. So I pushed ahead. It seemed I could hear every heartbeat as I made agonizingly slow progress.

Then, finally, I reached my wheelchair. I fell backward

into it and dropped the picture frame that I had used as a cane.

Now I could move. I lifted my shield briefly. Pain zapped me, and I dropped the shield back into place. That told me Luke Daab hadn't yet released the gas.

I pictured him at the far end of the dome, hooking up the tanks of poisonous gas to the vent system.

I pictured the gas seeping into the air, an invisible killer, making this a dome of death.

I pictured Ashley and all the other kids waking up in the morning, stepping outside of their sealed dorm and finding all the bodies of the adults—Mom and Rawling among them.

I pictured Luke Daab forcing us to assemble the carbon-dioxide generators. The Manchurian fleet landing. And the Manchurians forcing all of us robot-control kids into slavery.

How much time did I have left to stop the release of the gas?

And what would I do about it? I wondered about rolling through the dome to yell out a warning. However, there were nearly 200 adults now under the dome. Some were asleep. Some were working late or the night shift. No way would I be able to alert all of them, especially because Daab would hear me too. All he'd have to do was stun me with his neuron gun. In the confusion, he could slip away and return to the tanks of poisonous gas.

No, I'd have to stop Daab. But I was in a wheelchair. He was fully mobile and had a neuron gun.

Could Ashley help me? No, she was in the dorm. If I woke her and she opened the sealed entrance as the poisonous gas was released, all the kids would die too.

My thoughts spun wildly. What about somehow blocking

the vents so that poison gas wouldn't reach anyone? Too many vents.

God, help me! I begged, feeling desperate. Wasn't there some way I could stop Luke Daab—and save the lives of all the people on Mars? Not to mention the future possibility of more people who would be able to make Mars their new home?

A minute later the solution hit me.

I turned my wheelchair and pushed hard toward the computer room.

⚛

The first thing I did was go to the wall and pull down an oxygen tube. I strapped it to my face. If I ran out of time, I didn't want my own body collapsing from the poisonous gas before I could accomplish my mission.

Second, I connected my spinal plug to a computer transmitter.

I guessed I was down to a minute.

I didn't waste time putting on a helmet. I'd keep my eyes closed and concentrate as much as possible. It was something I'd learned to do in emergencies.

The connection to my robot hit, and with it came that familiar sensation of falling, falling, falling. . . .

⚛

Earlier, Ashley and I had moved our robots back from the surface of Mars to just inside the dome.

When the robot's visual lenses opened, they showed her robot parked beside mine.

I directed the robot to shoot forward.

Now it had to be down to seconds before the gas released.

My robot whirred through the dome. I cornered and hit two tekkies who were walking slowly, deep in conversation. They bounced off the robot body.

"Hey! Hey!" they shouted in anger.

I kept going. I would apologize to them later. *If* I succeeded in saving their lives along with all the other adults under the dome.

My robot crashed through some plants as I took a shortcut. A scientist yelled at me.

I kept going.

Was it my imagination, or had a green cloud just been released through the vents?

Go, go, go! I shouted in my mind.

Then I reached it. The place in the dome Daab had punctured earlier. A repair was in place, of course.

Short of a welding torch, there was only one way to break through.

And I had it. The power of a six-foot-tall titanium robot moving at close to 30 miles an hour.

I raised the right arm of the robot and stretched it out horizontally in front of me. Like a spear. I made a fist. I sped up the robot's wheels. And aimed.

The arm of the robot pierced the repair patch at top speed. As the titanium broke through, the robot body slammed into the wall of the dome. As it fell backward, half destroyed, I yelled *Stop!* and severed the connection between the robot and my own brain waves.

Although the video lenses no longer sent information to my brain, I didn't need the visuals of the robot to see if I had succeeded in puncturing the repair patch.

A great *whoosh* hit, as the atmosphere outside the dome began to suck out the air around me. It pulled a ribbon of green—the poisonous gas that had just started to settle downward toward the floor.

And best of all, the horns broke into full scream, sending an unmistakable warning to every person inside the dome to grab a nearby oxygen tube and strap it on.

All they would breathe until the poisonous gas cleared was life-giving oxygen.

EPILOGUE

07.30.2043

Three months have passed since Luke Daab's last stand—since he almost made the Mars Dome a place of death. That night, not a single person died.

Except maybe Luke himself.

He fled during the confusion, breaking out of the dome in his space suit, running toward the space shuttle.

We knew that by the footprints we followed the next day.

By then the shuttle was gone.

Maybe he'd hoped to connect with Dr. Jordan, the other Terratakers, and the Manchurian fleet. But only if his oxygen and water lasted.

If so, he hadn't planned on Rawling finding the surface-to-space missile triggers. Or the communications system software that Daab had hidden inside an empty oxygen tank.

So when the atomic weapons were ready and

the news was broadcast to Earth, the Manchurian fleet simply turned around. Who could blame them? Even Terratakers and Manchurians weren't stupid. They knew when they couldn't win.

As for Luke Daab? If he had planned to meet them in the middle of space, he'd gambled wrong. Because of it, his space shuttle probably had become a tomb that would drift forever in space.

I stopped writing in my diary to think about that for a minute. The very thought made me shiver. I wasn't sure if even a bad guy like Luke Daab deserved that kind of an end.

Then I smiled and continued writing my update.

As for me, Rawling had determined that the implant wasn't going to harm my spinal nerves. At least not for years. By then, he'd said, an Earth ship would be able to bring in one of the mini-robots capable of going into my bloodstream and working the nerves loose.

Was I walking yet?

Yes, slowly. But no one in the dome knew, because I'd been practicing secretly.

And I had my own plan to show it when the time was right.

Like tonight . . .

Midafternoon that day, the robots Ashley and I each controlled stood at the base of a great, gleaming copper globe, fully five stories above the surface of the red planet. We were surrounded by all the other robots controlled by the other kids. Even so, with nearly 50 robots in formation gathered at the base, the globe appeared overwhelmingly large.

Behind us were the dome's platform buggies. As many of the scientists and tekkies who could fit inside were staring upward at the carbon-dioxide generator as well.

Five minutes earlier, the robots had been swarming two half-assembled generators beside this one.

But the time had arrived—and nobody would be working for the rest of the afternoon.

After all of the equipment had been put aside and the noise from that died down, I could only hear the Martian wind—and the sand it carried, which tapped against the robots' titanium shells.

Dying sunlight bounced off the copper. Already stars were visible above the darkening horizon.

"This is it, Tyce. History."

"I am glad you are with me, Ashley."

It just seemed right, to be out here in the robots. And it made room for other people to be in the platform buggies.

Among them were Mom, Dad, and Rawling. None of us wanted to miss this.

Back at the dome, the chief engineer was activating the first carbon-dioxide generator. A little wisp of white cloud left the top of the copper globe. It was surprisingly undramatic.

"That's it?" Ashley's robot said to mine. "How is that going to fill the atmosphere with—"

Then a great mushroom of white rose higher and higher, growing wider and wider until it filled the sky above us. It would pour out this gas day after day, year after year, along with the five other generators that we'd been working so hard to assemble. And soon enough, the carbon dioxide—trapped by the thin Mars atmosphere that already existed—would begin to trap heat. It was a miracle—the way that it didn't just float off into space. Instead it stayed—and would enable plants to grow. Once plants could grow, they would produce oxygen. And in the meantime, it was enough hope for Earth to keep countries from going to war.

"Yeah," I replied to her robot. "I guess that is it. Think it will work?"

The white cloud above us meant that millions of people currently on Earth would live. And in the centuries to come, millions and millions and millions more would survive—and thrive. It didn't mean all our problems on Mars—or the Earth's problems—were magically over. There were still years of work ahead—through developing new scientific theories that would lead to bigger, better technology; faster ways to move people between Earth and Mars; ways to help them adjust to a new world. But there was hope now for the future of humankind—enough hope to keep the peace. And all of us kids had had a lot to do with generating that hope. It was something we could be proud of. Now some of the robot-control kids would choose to go back to Earth on the next spaceship, when Earth and Mars lined up in their closest orbits again. Others—like Ashley and me—could choose to stay. To make a place for ourselves and others in this exciting new world. A new world on a beautiful red planet.

Later, when the celebration at the dome quieted down, Ashley rolled me in my wheelchair to one of the garden spots. I'd asked her to take me there because of what I'd planned.

She stood beside my wheelchair, half covered with the shadows from the trees.

I rolled my wheelchair forward slightly to where I had hidden my comp-board, with its built-in DVD-gigarom player, beneath a bench.

I clicked a button. A quiet voice began to sing softly, with guitar as a background.

"What's this?" Ashley asked.

"An old ballad from Earth," I said. "About kids with hopes and dreams."

"I like it."

"Me too."

Then I stood up calmly . . . and walked toward Ashley.

"Tyce! You can . . . you can . . ." She wasn't able to finish as she began to cry with happiness for me.

"Yes, I can walk," I said.

I extended a hand. There had been something I'd been dreaming of doing for years. And I had practiced it over the last three months too. For hours with the song playing softly in my room.

"And there's something else I can do too." I smiled.

With a puzzled look on her face, Ashley took my hand.

"Care to dance?" I asked.

And so we did, with her tears falling freely on my shoulders.

WHAT'S THE MATTER WITH MATTER?

Did you know that, when it comes down to it, some people consider you just "one big chunk of matter"?

Well, they're partially right. After all, Tyce himself knew that "in the beginning moments of the universe, energy created matter and antimatter."

Sounds easy, huh? But here's what's the matter with matter: when matter and antimatter touch, *bam!* They explode, destroying each other. You see, matter is made up of what's called *quarks;* antimatter is made of *antiquarks.* Although quarks and antiquarks are identical to each other in most aspects, their touching and the subsequent explosion results in a burst of energy.

Physicists tell us that in the first moments of creation, the energy levels were so high that immediately upon self-destruction, new quarks and antiquarks were formed. But as the universe began to cool, there was no way for new quarks and antiquarks to replace the destroyed ones.

Basically all this technical stuff means that, according to the laws of physics, nothing in this universe should exist.

And that means no Moon, no sun, no Mars, no Earth. And certainly no you.

Instead, for reasons physicists can't figure out, for every 10 billion antiquarks, the beginning universe created 10 billion and one quarks. And that one extra quark per every 10 billion antiquarks led to an infinite amount of matter that became the planets, stars, and galaxies of the universe.

So how is it that so much matter managed to survive? Why is there some matter rather than no matter?

Science cannot give us that answer. In fact, the chances that matter could survive are, according to a bigwig Oxford mathematician, Roger Penrose, less than one in 10^{123}. That's a 10 followed by 123 zeros, which means the chances are not likely at all!

Yet somehow, against those kinds of odds, the universe grew in a way to make life possible on Earth. To make *your* life possible.

No matter what, many scientists argue that this shows us that the creation of the universe was not a random event. Our bodies are composed of the dust of the stars. The carbon and hydrogen and oxygen and trace elements are arranged in such a way that we can breathe, that our eyes can interpret light waves, and that our brains can generate thoughts and give instructions to our bodies (much as Tyce's brain waves tell the robot how to move in this story).

When you think about this, it's not so startling to think that the world was not only created, but it continues to spin and move at the direction of an invisible Creator. A Creator who exists beyond what we can see and sometimes sense physically. A Creator who sustains us through daily miracles. Like the fact that the sunlight is not too strong and not too weak. It comes from a star the perfect distance away from Earth in order to allow plants to grow in the dirt that was once stardust. Not only do our bodies depend on these plants, we find nutrition in the protein of animals that eat these plants.

The life cycle of all matter on this planet exists because of things like this—sunlight, water, and dirt—all possible because of the creation events set in motion by God at the beginning of time. It's that simple. And also that wonderful.

So in the end, science can't totally answer the question of "what's the matter with matter?"

But God can. And everything you learn about science will only strengthen the ability of your brain to accept his existence. Even when things seem impossible (like the reaction of matter and antimatter), God will always find a way.

ABOUT THE AUTHOR

Sigmund Brouwer, his wife, recording artist Cindy Morgan, and their daughter split living between Red Deer, Alberta, Canada, and Nashville, Tennessee. He has written several series of juvenile fiction and eight novels. Sigmund loves sports and plays golf and hockey. He also enjoys visiting schools to talk about books. He welcomes visitors to his Web site at www.coolreading.com, where he and a bunch of other authors like to hang out in cyberspace.

MARS DIARIES

are you ready?

Set in an experimental community on Mars in the years 2039–2043, the Mars Diaries feature teen virtual-reality specialist Tyce Sanders. Life on the red planet is not always easy, but it is definitely exciting. As Tyce explores his strange surroundings, he also finds that the mysteries of the planet point to his greatest discovery—a new relationship with God.

MISSION 1: Oxygen Level Zero
Time was running out...

MISSION 2: Alien Pursuit
"Help me!" And the radio went dead....

MISSION 3: Time Bomb
A quake rocks the red planet, uncovering a long kept secret....

MISSION 4: Hammerhead
I was dead center in the laser target controls....

MISSION 5: Sole Survivor
Scientists buried alive at cave-in site!

MISSION 6: Moon Racer
Everyone has a motive...and secrets. The truth must be found before it's too late.

MISSION 7: Countdown
20 soldiers, 20 neuron rifles. There was nowhere to run. Nowhere to hide...

MISSION 8: Robot War
Ashley and I are their only hope, and they think we're traitors.

MISSION 9: Manchurian Sector
I was in trouble...and I couldn't trust anyone.

MISSION 10: Last Stand
Invasion was imminent ... and we'd lost all contact with Earth.

COOL
2
READ
.com